Wed to the Wrong Wexford

Laura Osborne

Other Works by Laura Osborne:

The Lady's Masked Mistake

His Lordship's Star-Crossed Lady

Seducing Her Husband

Regaining the Love of a Duke

Wed to the Wrong Wexford

Laura Osborne

DEDICATION

For Fran,

Words cannot describe how much you mean to me and the gang

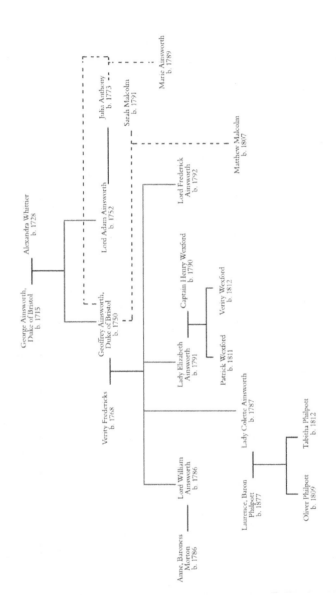

Laura Osborne

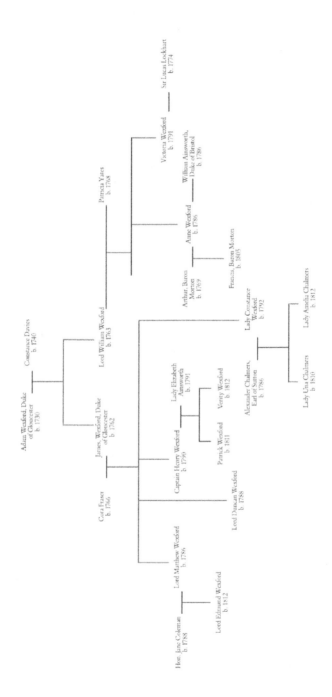

Adam Wexford, Duke of Gloucester b. 1730 — Constance Davies b. 1740

James, Wexford, Duke of Gloucester b. 1762 — Cara Fraser b. 1766

Lord William Wexford b. 1763 — Patricia Yates b. 1768

Victoria Wexford b. 1791 — Sir Lucas Lockhart b. 1774

Anne Wexford b. 1786 — William Ainsworth, Duke of Bristol b. 1786

Arthur, Baron Morton b. 1769 — Francis, Baron Morton b. 1805

Captain Henry Wexford b. 1790 — Lady Elizabeth Ainsworth b. 1791

Lord Matthew Wexford b. 1786 — Hon. Jane Coleman b. 1788

Lord Duncan Wexford b. 1788

Lady Constance Wexford b. 1792 — Alexander Chalmers, Earl of Sutton b. 1786

Patrick Wexford b. 1811

Verity Wexford b. 1812

Lord Edmund Wexford b. 1812

Lady Una Chalmers b. 1810

Lady Amelia Chalmers b. 1812

Wed to the Wrong Wexford

Prologue

The trials and tribulations of a girl's first love

Miss Caroline Morton was just shy of her tenth birthday when her beloved father, Baron Morton, sat her and her younger sister down for a serious discussion.

The brunette Caroline and blonde Wilhelmina listened as their Papa informed them that he was engaged to be wed. The sisters exchanged a glance, asked some cursory questions about their prospective stepmother, and wished their father happiness.

Upon leaving their Papa, the pair went to sit in their nursery to discuss the surprising news. Caroline listened as her sister declared herself to be looking forward to having a new mother.

Wilhelmina's sentiments were not in agreement with her own.

Caroline could hardly blame her sister, of course, though Wilhelmina was only two years younger than herself, those years made all the difference when it came to possessing memories of their late mother.

Mary Morton had passed away five years prior and, though her memories of her were few, Caroline had always remembered her mother with love and missed her very much.

Nevertheless, she also loved her father and wanted the Baron to be happy as well, in addition to being well aware that, as girls, she and her sister could not inherit his title, and so a little brother would regretfully be needed. So, Caroline decided that she would be warm and welcoming to Miss Anne Wexford, if a little wary.

The girl could not deny being impressed at how her future stepmother appeared determined to include the sisters in all her activities. Especially as the woman was preparing a wedding in the short space of three weeks, which Caroline assumed meant that there would be no time for them.

It also helped the girl that Anne was a mere eight years older than herself, making her seem somewhat relatable to the sisters.

The three weeks passed by in a blur and, the next thing Caroline knew, she was dressed in a new frock and walking down the aisle to watch her Papa wed.

The wedding was a small affair, and Caroline stared at her new stepmother's family out of the corner of her eye during the ceremony. She had been told that Anne was the niece of a duke, leading Caroline to somewhat naively assume that the entire Wexford family would be rather gluttonous and uppity, but she was pleased to observe that they did not appear so.

She had met her stepmother's parents and sister whilst the wedding was being planned, so paid no mind to them. It was the group of six in the row behind that truly sparked her interest.

The Duke and Duchess were a rather handsome couple, Caroline thought, and she imagined the Duchess in particular, with her black hair and green eyes, to look somewhat exotic. In fact, Caroline realised, she looked almost exactly like a woman from a picture in one of her books about Spain.

The woman's looks had clearly been passed onto her daughter, who sat beside her. The girl, Constance, was scarcely older than Caroline, but she felt somewhat childish, and inferior compared to the poised little lady she saw.

Next to her was the tallest of the three boys in the row, leading Caroline to deduce him to be the eldest son, Matthew. Like his mother and sister, he possessed striking raven black hair but lacked a certain softness compared to them. In fact, she decided that the young man looked much too serious for her liking.

Next to him was also the next tallest in height, therefore he was probably Duncan. Whilst Caroline thought he seemed much friendlier than his brother, he was not nearly as handsome, and Caroline thought that he was only a handful of cakes away from being what she politely referred to as 'jolly'. This one had the chestnut brown locks of his father, instead, though he had inherited his mother's green eyes.

Eyes, which Caroline realised, were now focused entirely upon her. She froze for a moment, but a lopsided smile and a wink caused her to quickly face the front, her cheeks aflame.

She did not dare risk another glance for the entire ceremony, leaving the third and final Wexford brother a mystery. Upon leaving the church, she stared ahead the entire time, and swore she heard a boyish chuckle behind her.

The wedding breakfast was hosted at Anne's childhood home and her new stepmother was keen to introduce the girls to her young cousin.

Despite being ever so prim and proper, Caroline decided that Connie, as she preferred to be called, was actually quite a lot of fun and seemed to enjoy relentlessly mocking her brothers.

Caroline found this especially wonderful as the brother who would not leave them alone, and so was the prime target of his sister's ire, was Duncan Wexford himself. Even more infuriating was how the boy appeared to be determined to tease Caroline as best he could.

After almost twenty minutes of being subjected to the fifteen-year old's teasing, Caroline was very close to embarrassing herself in front of her new relatives by delivering him a blow to the head.

She was prevented from doing so, however, by a voice from behind her. A voice that would have the greatest impact on her thus far in her near ten-year life.

"I thought you knew how to charm girls?"

Caroline turned around and promptly fell in love with Lord Henry Wexford.

Like his irritating brother, Harry had brown locks and green eyes, but Caroline thought they suited him far more. He exuded a sense of confidence and light-heartedness that charmed her completely.

Soon enough, Caroline could do nothing but stare at him like a love-sick puppy. Unfortunately for her, everyone noticed.

The only teasing she had to endure over it was from her sister, who told her time and time again over the next weeks, months, and years that a fourteen-year-old boy would want nothing to do with a ten-year-old girl following after him.

The ages in the teasing phrase changed as time went on.

Caroline was not naïve enough to believe that her devotion Harry would mean he was not subject to teasing himself. In fact, she even overheard some of it herself.

Duncan, naturally, was bullying her beloved relentlessly over her and even sought to call her some choice names. Harry's only reaction was to defend her honour, and fought his brother, winning and making him swear not to make fun of Caroline again.

This only made her love him even more.

Over the years, circumstance kept them apart, but Caroline's feelings only grew.

Almost exactly one year after the wedding, she received the much sought-after brother. His sisters thought Francis to be odd-looking when they first met, but the girls soon saw him grow into his looks.

Tragically, not three years later, their beloved Papa died suddenly. Naturally, Caroline was distraught. Though she considered Anne a mother, the love and comfort she provided could not distract the girl from the fact that she was now an orphan.

A month after the sad affair, however, a letter arrived in the post addressed to Miss Caroline Morton. Confused, she tore it open, and her heart began to pound as she read the words of sympathy from her beloved Harry.

Caroline's heart soared and she began to feel as though there might be more hope for life than she had first thought. Even more consuming was the final line in the letter:

If you ever find yourself in need of a friend, trust that I shall always be here for you.

Why else should Harry make such a declaration if he did not feel the same, Caroline thought. She was now surer than ever that one day she would be Lady Henry Wexford.

The news shortly after of Harry having enlisted in the British Army brought Caroline back to despair. It was made even worse by how Anne refused to have them leave their Suffolk home for London.

Try as she might, Caroline could not convince her Mama to change her mind, and the cried herself to sleep imagining her handsome love being struck down before they could declare their feelings for one another and share at least one perfect kiss.

A little over a year later, the now-sixteen-year-old actually fainted upon hearing that he would be returning from the continent. She could not determine, however, if her rather over the top reaction was because she knew he would be coming home safe or the fact that he had been so injured from battle that he would be returning sans half a leg.

Knowing that her love would be in London during the next season, Caroline begged her Mama to allow her to make her debut, but it was to no avail. For some strange reason, Anne had decided that they would remain in mourning indefinitely, postponing her debut.

Nonetheless, Caroline reassured herself, Harry would wait for her.

He did not.

January 1811 brought about the news that shattered Caroline's heart into a million pieces. He had eloped with Lady Elizabeth Ainsworth.

Caroline knew next to nothing of the woman who had stolen her beloved's heart. One thing she did know, however, was that the harridan was a member of a family that loathed the Wexfords so she was sure that Harry would not have gone into marriage without being forced to.

Caroline spent the following months despondent. It appeared that, no matter what solution she considered, none would lead to a happy ending for the pair. She had even considered offering herself to Harry as a mistress, but the ruination that would bring to her family stopped her from enacting that idea.

As the years went on, she grew resigned to her fate, and when the time came that Anne decided it was time to return to London for her debut, Caroline was prepared to make a loveless marriage.

But she knew that her heart would never forget the man with the chestnut locks and green eyes.

Chapter One

"The game is exceptional in the Autumn months. I imagine you shall find it so yourself."

Caroline's mouth was already beginning to ache from the smile she had fixed upon it. She could not believe this was only her third dance of the night, it felt like her fiftieth!

She had a brief respite before having to answer her partner, but once the steps required that she must face him again, Caroline was forced to continue what she thought was a rather strained conversation. Even though Mr Woodward did not appear to realise so.

"I doubt I shall find myself visiting your grandfather's estate in the Autumn, sir."

"I think the chances of your doing so are much greater than you believe." He beamed, refusing to either be put off or take the hint.

He thinks I should feel honoured he has taken a fancy!

Caroline was thankful that they had to move away from each other once more and happened to step beside her sister as she did so.

"Your Sir Ernest had best propose soon," she said through gritted teeth, "or else I shall flee back home on my own."

The involuntary snort that her sister let out cheered Caroline up immensely. Even better was the look of horror that she made in reaction.

Wilhelmina did not have the opportunity to offer a retort, as they moved apart, forcing the older girl to return to her dance partner.

Though there were only a few bars remaining, Caroline knew she should give her partner her entire attention. However, a pair of emerald green eyes spotted over Mr Woodward's shoulder took over her mind entirely.

For a moment, she felt her heart begin to pound in her chest and her breath quickened. Then it was over, and Caroline remembered that the man she was thinking of was not partaking in this season.

She was still unsure if she was relieved or disappointed over that fact.

Looking back at the spot, Caroline tried not to grimace upon seeing that the man she considered both her tormentor and her confidant was gazing at her with a delighted smirk on his face. One that she knew would be causing her to suffer in a few moments.

Finally, the music came to an end. Demurely curtseying to her partner, she reluctantly allowed him to take her arm in his and escort her off the dance floor.

"Might I be so forward as to write my name on your dance card again this evening?" Mr Woodward asked, mistaken confidence exuding from his form. "I would very much desire to dance a waltz with you, Miss Morton."

Realising that she had one free waltz remaining on her dance card, Caroline panicked, having no desire to dance with the poor man ever again.

"I regret that my card is full for that particular dance." she hastily answered. "Perhaps at the next ball we both find ourselves attending?"

Refusing to wait for a response, she made up some excuse over needing to speak to her mother and rushed away, not daring to look back to the man.

Surprisingly, Caroline found it almost impossible to find the woman in question, having scoured the ballroom with no trace whatsoever of her Mama.

Frowning, she stood beside a pillar, thankful that she was not so popular that she could not pass as a wallflower. Once she resolved to come away from her hiding place, she would transform back into a somewhat-dazzling debutante.

Caroline mentally retraced her steps, trying to think of where she last saw her mother. After arriving with Anne and Wilhelmina, both girls had quickly been asked to dance, and she realised with horror that she had not seen the woman since. It was of the utmost importance that she find her at once, lest gossip began over the girls losing their chaperone.

Just as she decided to do another sweep of the room, Caroline let out a squeak of surprise upon having a glass of lemonade suddenly appear in front of her face.

Jumping back against the pillar, Caroline desired nothing more in that moment than to hit Duncan Wexford over the head. Especially upon seeing how amused her was at her reaction.

"I said that you looked parched." he grinned, indicating his head to the glass.

"How thoughtful of you." Caroline sarcastically replied, earning a mocking bow from him. She took the glass from his hands and drained it in record speed before shoving it back at him. Without missing a beat, Duncan deposited the glass behind the pillar.

"I should have known you were so uncouth that you do not have the manners to put it back where you found it." She remarked.

"You know," Duncan said, moving to stand beside her, facing the crowd, "I think this may be my favourite season I have partaken in."

"I wonder why."

"Seeing you having to go against your better nature and be polite to all those gentlemen is particularly entertaining."

"What makes you think I am feigning how I behave with the gentlemen? Is it so impossible to think that I may enjoy their company?"

"Caro," he said, seriously, "anyone who knows you can tell when your smile is forced. Besides, I do not think you could have run away fast enough from your last dance partner. If I did not feel so sorry for the man, I would have laughed at how he stared in wonder after you."

Caroline crinkled her nose in disgust at that.

"I actually was trying to find Mama, have you seen her?"

"No." Duncan did a cursory glance around the room before repeating his answer. She let out a sigh.

"Buck up, little one, I am sure there is another young man searching for you to sweep into his arms for the next dance."

"Wonderful." she dryly responded. "What even is the next dance?"

"A waltz, I believe."

It took Caroline a moment to understand the implication of his words. Panicking she forcibly moved him so that his back faced the ballroom and thrust her wrist in his face.

"What on ear......"

"Sign your name to the next waltz on my card." she whispered sternly.

"Why should I do that?"

"Because I said my waltzes were all taken. Now sign it."

"For god's sake, Caroline. Who did you lie to this time?" He moaned about it, but Caroline did not fail to see that he signed his name.

"Mr Woodward."

Though he said nothing, it was clear from Duncan's face that Caroline was about to spend the next dance being chastised.

Where the devil is Anne?

The question kept running through Duncan's mind during the first minute of the dance. He kept scouring the crowd to try and find his missing cousin but no trace of her could be found. Knowing how dependable the woman was, he was beginning to worry that something had happened.

"Really, Duncan, one would think that dancing with me was the most unbearable experience."

He looked down at Caroline to see a teasing smirk on her face, which made him feel a little more relaxed.

"You know well enough that we should not be dancing together." he scolded.

"And why is that? We are cousins, there is nothing wrong with us partaking in a waltz together."

Duncan mentally groaned at her stubbornness. Now was most certainly not the time for it.

"Firstly, I am cousins with your stepmother, not you. Society does not see us as related and, even if it did, being cousins would hardly matter in that department."

Caroline opened her mouth to protest so Duncan sent her a look to tell her to not even try.

"And secondly, you were at the concert the other night and heard Anne say that my being around you girls was inappropriate just as well as I heard it. I would think you would understand how serious that particular argument is."

"Oh please, anyone with any sense knows that you would never take liberties with unwed maidens. You prefer an experienced woman as Mama says. Whatever that means."

Duncan sighed as he realised that the girl in his arms was not going to take his point seriously.

"I can see at least three people in my line of sight who are looking at us disapprovingly." He lowered his voice then. "I imagine this is especially bad because we do not know where your chaperone is."

It appeared he was finally getting through to her, as Caroline's eyes narrowed as she thought over his warnings. If there was one thing Duncan had learned over the past decade of knowing the girl, it was how to read her expressions and he was almost certain she was giving his words some serious thought.

Realising that they were only halfway through the waltz, he decided to change the subject, lest he would be subjected to a moody Caroline for another few minutes. A most terrifying prospect.

"What is wrong with the young man, anyway?" he asked, causing her to gaze up at him with a questioning look. "The one you were trying to avoid. I am sure he is respectable."

Caroline sighed. "Respectable, he is. Wealthy also. He seems kind and I suppose he could be considered handsome but there is just something missing."

"Well, I am sure that there are others who would be more appealing to dance with than this old fool." Duncan beamed upon hearing her responding laughter.

"Is four and twenty considered old now? You are not even considered old enough to marry."

"I shall be five and twenty in a week, you forget, and the men in my family have all married younger. In any case, you are ignoring my point entirely."

Caroline twisted her mouth in annoyance, which only served to amuse Duncan further.

"If you must know," she began, "I find them all lacking. I keep telling myself that I should not expect to find a husband who makes me weak at the knees. But whenever I try to give them a chance, I am just........." He felt her hands stretch as her voice trailed off.

Duncan felt a pang of sympathy for the girl as she tried to put into words how she felt. When his sister had her first season, he could remember thinking that the man she thought she was going to marry just did not bring out the spark in his little Connie that he knew so well.

As luck would have it, she had ended up having to marry someone completely different. As angry as Duncan had been over the entire situation, he could never deny that Sutton was the perfect match for her.

It served to make him feel more thankful that, as a man, he did not need to find a spouse to settle for. Of course, that made him feel more sorry for the girl in his arms.

"Chin up, Caro," he said, "I would wager that you will be swept off your feet when you least expect it."

"Hmmmm." was her only response.

"You should believe me. After all, I am older and wiser than you."

Duncan inwardly celebrated as a disbelieving smile began to appear on Caroline's face and her eyes lit up in challenge.

"I was under the impression that I would have to be a fool to believe any word you said."

"I will have you know," he retorted, "that I am a rake, not a liar. I should thank you to know the difference."

"Either way, I should consider you one of the most untrustworthy people I have the misfortune of knowing."

Just as Duncan opened his mouth to respond, he realised the music was coming to a close and found himself now actually rather sorry that the dance was about to end. He always enjoyed a good sparring match with the girl.

Mockingly bowing at her, he took her arm in his and escorted her off the dance floor. Anne was still nowhere to be found, but he could see his brother's wife, Jane, gesturing to them and so led the way over to her.

"I am afraid that your mother has a headache and has left me in charge of the two of you." she explained.

"I assume you are referring to Wilhelmina instead of me." he quipped, resulting in an irritated look being directed his way.

"Miss Morton, I believe you promised me this dance."
A young man whom Duncan did not know interrupted them.
He had not realised her arm was still in his until she pulled it
away.

With barely another word or glance, Caroline left to
return to the dancefloor. Duncan was surprised at the
resulting stab of irritation in his gut at the young buck.

Turning back to Jane, he studied the redhead.

"Are you going to tell me what actually happened to
Anne?"

Her head pulled back in surprise, and she asked his
meaning.

"Dear Janey, you forget that no one has ever thought
you a good actress." He lifted his eyebrows in amusement, and
she shook her head at him.

"You shall find out soon enough." she said before
walking off to speak with her other charge for the night.

Contemplating what her words could mean, Duncan
looked about the room, needing to find some new
entertainment.

His eyes then met a pair of light blue ones, and he was
rather pleased to find that they belonged to the wife of a
particularly odious poet often seen at his club. Even better was
the clear invitation on her face.

With one final glance towards the dancefloor, Duncan made his way towards what he thought would be a much more pleasant experience.

Chapter Two

To describe Caroline as furious would perhaps be an understatement.

She had been the perfectly behaved debutante all night and was ready to recount the experience to her mother at the breakfast table. After enquiring after her health, of course.

The second Anne had stepped through the doorway to the breakfast room, however, she knew that something was wrong. What her mother had revealed, though, was nothing that Caroline could ever imagine.

And so, she had retreated to her room as soon as she could, claiming the need to ready for the day. Caroline was unsure, however, if she would ever be ready to face today.

"I cannot believe she could be so foolish to do such a thing!" she cried out, realising too late that she had slammed her bedroom door in her sister's face.

Re-opening it, Caroline gave her sister an apologetic grimace, which the younger girls thankfully accepted.

"It is hardly as though Mama has a choice."
Wilhelmina argued, taking a seat on her sister's bed.

Said sister was now pacing the room, muttering curses under her breath.

"Come along, Caro, you know she would never have agreed to it otherwise."

"She still landed herself in this situation." the brunette spat out in return. "It is entirely her fault."

"I think that the blame is shared with a certain someone else." Caroline heard her sister mutter and turned to her with a somewhat deranged look upon her face.

"I do not care what role that man had to play!" she declared. "Mama knows that any decisions she makes affects the three of us. She should have thought about her children when she went off and compromised herself with *Liam Ainsworth!*"

Once her outburst was finished, all Caroline saw in her sister's eyes were of sympathy and all her anger began to recede as despair took its place.

Dropping into the spot next to Wilhelmina, she did her utmost not to let the threatening tears out.

"I understand this must be difficult for you, Caro."

"We shall have to live with him, Mina. In a house surrounded by portraits and memories of his family. And we shall have to spend time with them also."

As Caroline stared down at her clenched hands, she felt an arm wrap around her, and a head come to rest upon her shoulder.

"I thought I could avoid seeing them." she whispered out. "I imagined that I would find myself a husband who would whisk me away before they ever came out of mourning."

"You can still do that, Caro."

"Can I?" Caroline turned to face the younger girl, uncaring that the tears were flowing freely down her face now. "Mama will be one of them. If I hide away, I shall have lost two mothers. That prospect is even more terrifying."

She watched as her sister chewed on her bottom lip, contemplating what to say next.

"You could not avoid it forever." she finally said. "At least you shall be able to prepare yourself."

"I do not think I shall ever be prepared for it."

"You know this how? Remember when Papa died? Grandmama told us that, no matter how much it hurt at the time, it would get easier. And she was right in the end."

Caroline let out a sniffle as her sister continued. "Besides, as long as you run away and hide from them, you are always making it worse in your head." Wilhelmina smiled. "I am almost certain that you will be surprised at how little effect they have on you."

"I have imagined it a thousand times." Caroline whispered. "Each time is worse than the last. If he is miserable with her, then I am sad for him. If she is the miserable one, then I am sad because he has to suffer through not having his feelings returned. Or worse......"

She refused to voice that particular fear. Seeing her beloved Harry unhappy would devastate her. But the thought of having to witness him be happy with his wife.... Caroline did not think she could ever cope with seeing that.

"Then we shall have to do more to find you a husband." her sister declared, prompting Caroline to roll her eyes.

"I think the men we have encountered already this season is enough indication that that wish is not coming true."

"For one thing, it is not a wish, it is a task I am setting for myself."

"And for another?" Caroline teased, resulting in a mischievous smile to appear on Wilhelmina's face.

"We have help now." Upon seeing her sister's confused look, the younger girl explained. "Ernest and I are practically engaged; I shall get him to find the best prospects for you amongst his cohorts."

"Meaning I would never be able to escape you, if our husbands are friends."

"Precisely." Wilhelmina nodded. "Besides, even if Ernest cannot find the perfect man for you, I imagine the list of available men is about to become longer for you."

"And why should you imagine that?" Caroline asked, though she did not think she wished to hear the answer.

"Mama is going to marry one of the richest men in the country, from one of the oldest families to boot. Gentlemen from far and wide are going to be falling over themselves to ask for your hand."

Turning her head away, Caroline stared ahead, her mouth agape.

"Does that mean what I think it does?" She did not need to look at her sister to know that Wilhelmina was enthusiastically nodding her head.

"Most assuredly. Caroline darling, from the second this engagement is announced, you are going to become the most eligible lady in all of England."

Caroline was suddenly thankful that she had eaten very little for breakfast.

That day, Duncan did not rise until after noon. He was rather disappointed to have discovered his bed mate already vanished, for he would have enjoyed having one more tup before rising.

Deciding to not waste the day entirely, tempting though it was, he opted to go on a walk, and found his feet had unconsciously led him to the front steps of Wexford House.

Not bothering to wait to be announced, he strode into the drawing room where he found his parents entertaining half the family.

"Well," he said to the room, "I see that Harry and I are clearly not your favourites."

"Not since you lost your status as Matt's heir." his sister smirked, prompting Duncan to impishly poke his tongue out at her.

With a prolonged sigh, he threw himself into the chaise beside her in an exaggerated motion and was almost instantly told by his mother to sit up straight.

With a grumble, he complied, then asked what they were talking about before he arrived.

"If you must know, we were speaking of the children." his older brother commented.

"Oh god!" Duncan groaned. "I always forget how dull the rest of you are."

"I suppose that is further confirmation that I should not expect any news from you then?" his mother asked.

"Do any of us really want Duncan to marry and have children?" Jane asked, earning confused looks from the room.

"I just mean that we already see how whiny the man is. Imagine *that* after having children."

Before Duncan even had a chance to defend himself, his father added to the teasing.

"I do not think we should even discuss it. Knowing our luck, we would end up willing it into existence."

"If I did not know it would reduce Mama into a puddle of hysterical tears, I would wed just to spite you all."

"Do you know, I was thinking of this the other day." The Duchess started with a smile.

"Oh good," Duncan muttered as she continued on, "we are not giving up on the subject after all."

"Do not fret, brother dear," Connie said as she patted the top of his head, "we shall move onto other ways to mock you soon."

"I am not a dog." he complained at the gesture. Connie only shrugged in response.

As Duncan did his utmost to indulge on all the cakes within arm's length, he half-listened to his mother's newest thoughts on his hypothetical marriage. Apparently, the idea of him finally giving in and marrying was such an unlikely prospect that his mother planned to arrange the most lavish wedding in the history of London.

Soon enough, the rest of the family were chiming in with suggestions on how to make the event even more extravagant.

As he listened to his brother describe the entirely white ensemble that he would have to wear as groom, Duncan watched as his parents' butler, Jennings, walked in carrying the evening paper on a tray.

On a normal day, he would wordlessly hold the tray for the Duke to take the paper, and immediately leave. Unless his father had something to say, of course.

Today, however, Duncan was rather intrigued to see the man lean down and whisper in his father's ear. The Duke nodded and mumbled something his middle son could not make out, and then opened the paper, seemingly in search of a specific page. When he finally seemed to settle on said page, his eyebrows lifted in surprise.

"What is it?" Duncan asked his father, interrupting some suggestion Jane was making about an elephant.

The room turned silent as each person's eyes turned in the same direction as Duncan's own and they saw the serious look on the Duke's face.

"There is quite the announcement here. I imagine all of London will be abuzz by the end of the day."

"What is it, darling?"

"It seems the Duke of Bristol is engaged." That surprised Duncan, as far as he was aware, the man had practically become a hermit to avoid having to act the bereaved son and there were no rumblings about a lady before the old Duke had passed.

"Liam?" he heard Connie say to his side, surprise evident in her voice. That was telling, as her husband was one of the new Duke's closest confidants. If Connie did not know, it was certainly sudden and scandalous.

"Has Xander said anything about a secret courtship?" Matt asked her.

Connie shook her head. "Not at all. Who is he marrying, Papa?"

Their father looked around the room before answering, his expression rather uncertain. Duncan began to feel something form in the pit of his stomach in anticipation.

"The Dowager Baroness Morton."

For a moment, no one reacted. Even Duncan was so stupefied by what he had heard that he could not utter one snarky comment.

It was his brother that finally broke the silence.

"Anne?"

Their father nodded in confirmation.

"Our cousin Anne?"

Another nod.

"Uncle William's daughter, Anne?"

"Really, Matt." Connie said. "How many Anne's do we know who also happen to have that title and are our cousin?"

"Forgive me for needing to confirm it for my brain to fully comprehend whatever is going on." came the defensive reply.

A sudden thought came to Duncan as his siblings continued to bicker and his eyes narrowed onto a suspiciously silent redhead.

"Janey." he said, his voice teasing. An awkward smile graced his lips as he gritted out his following words. "Why did Anne leave the ball early last night?"

Four heads turned to stare at the woman who was now staring daggers at her brother-in-law, not that Duncan cared.

"Jane?" her husband asked. Looking at him, her face began to scrunch up as she cringed.

"She may have been discovered in an unexplainable position with the Duke."

Duncan could not help it. He burst into a bellowing laugh at her phrasing.

"I think it might be quite explainable, judging by how red your face is."

As he continued to laugh, Duncan heard his brother say his sister's name, and his head was suddenly pushed forward by the force of her palm colliding with the back of her head.

"Well, you cannot deny that it is unexpected. Who would have thought that Anne of all people.......?"

"Even so," his mother started, "I am sure your cousin is horrified by what has taken place, however scandalous it may be. I cannot think of anyone less inclined to hold such a high-ranking position in society."

"I imagine Wilhelmina will be a little put out." Connie remarked. "She has been anticipating a proposal but a sudden marriage for her mother may push it back."

"Oh my." the Duchess exclaimed. "You do not think the family shall have to go back into mourning, do you?"

"Why should they? They did not know old Ainsworth."

Mourning or not, Duncan thought, the entire Morton family was about to face a major upheaval. He was sure that most of the family would be fine with the changes once the shock wore off.

The realisation that a certain member would become despondent at these new events and give him even more prompts for teasing than before had Duncan rubbing his hands in gleeful anticipation.

Connie noticed and asked him what he was thinking. A beaming smile dominating his face, Duncan looked at his sister and uttered one word in explanation.

"Caroline."

A mixture of moans and sounds of pity erupted about the room.

"That poor girl." he heard his mother say.

She will be once I am done with her!

Chapter Three

Three days later, tensions in the Morton household were beginning to loosen.

The shock of the news had not entirely dissipated, but the mother and children were gradually becoming accustomed to the prospect of relocating to the Kensington home of Anne's intended.

Though Caroline had not quite forgiven her mother, she was understanding and so resolved not to hold it against the woman.

"Why are we not having a larger wedding?" she heard her sister ask from across the parlour, where the three women were waiting for lunch to be announced.

"If you must marry him, you could at least take advantage of how rich he is." Caroline grumbled. She received a pointed look from her mother in response. "Sorry Mama, I forgot that you are a better person than I am."

"For one thing, Wilhelmina, Liam is still in mourning, and so anything interpreted as opulent could be seen as crass and disrespectful."

Hearing the man's name from Anne's mouth was still something that Caroline was not yet used to.

"Besides, I prefer it to be a private event. I often find having to entertain large groups exhausting."

"You might find being a Duchess a chore then." Wilhelmina commented, earning an accidental whine from their mother.

"Mama!" Caroline jested. "One would think you are finding your impending nuptials to be a chore. I thought you were supposed to be the picture of blissful happiness."

"That is reserved for unwed maidens, not widows." Anne snarked back. "I must remember to tease you about such things when you become engaged."

"At least she has plenty of time to practice." Wilhelmina added. "We shall not have time for another wedding this season after my own."

"You are not even engaged!" Caroline balked.

"I am as good as."

Anne lifted her hands up to halt the coming sisterly war.

"Please girls, can we not find a topic of discussion that will not devolve into bickering?" she pleaded.

Caroline saw her sister give their Mama a confused look.

"We are sisters." she answered. "Half of our conversations end with us bickering."

Caroline nodded her head in agreement, though she was half tempted to disagree to prove her sister's point further.

"Can we at least try?" Anne pleaded, pinching the bridge of her nose. Caroline felt a twinge of sympathy. As much as her mother's actions were of her own doing, she was expected to continue chaperoning the two girls in addition to planning her wedding in the space of a month.

And then she would have to do it all over again when Sir Ernest inevitably proposed to Wilhelmina!

"When are we expected at the dressmaker?" she asked with a sigh, earning a grateful smile from her mother.

"We have an appointment on Tuesday, whilst there I shall enquire with Madame Angelique about making our gowns for the wedding."

"I still do not understand why we need new dresses." Caroline bemoaned. "We already have an entire new wardrobe."

"Just because you find dress shopping tedious, Caro, it does not mean that the rest of us do."

"I must find a way to feel superior to the rest of you." Caroline jested, sending her sister a wink.

Before the conversation could delve into an inevitable round of bickering, they were interrupted by the arrival of a footman. No doubt Anne was relieved at the man's appearance.

Surprisingly, he had not arrived to announce that luncheon was ready.

"Lord Duncan Wexford, My Lady."

He stepped aside to allow the man in question to enter the room. One look from the man filled Caroline with dread.

"NO!" she shouted before he even had a chance to greet them.

"*Caroline!*" her mother scolded. Caroline turned to the woman and pleaded.

"He is only here to tease me! You must not let him, Mama."

"Miss Morton, you wound me." Duncan mockingly placed his hand over his heart.

"Are we now pretending that you do not use any excuse to tease me whenever we speak?"

"At least give me a chance to make the proper greetings before I proceed in my true purpose for being here."

With that, he strode over to Anne and greeted her with a kiss on the cheek. He then moved to sit next to Wilhelmina, whom he also greeted with a kiss.

"Now, onto the true purpose for my visit today: Congratulations, Anne. You have done rather well for yourself."

Caroline pouted as she listened to Duncan spout off declarations over how wonderfully Anne had done for herself and her children. In return, she asked that another place be set for luncheon, causing Caroline's nostrils to flare in irritation.

Her irritation was increased during the quarter of an hour they spent waiting for the meal to be announced as Duncan had apparently decided that it would be more amusing to ignore Caroline entirely than make any teasing remarks.

If she were willing to admit it to herself, she also found it rather unnerving to not be the object of Duncan's attentions for the first time. For as long as she could remember, he had always focused upon mocking her when they were in one another's presence.

Caroline did not know what to do with the sudden privacy.

As the four finally made their way into the breakfast room for luncheon, she felt a dark presence come beside her and a glance sideways told her that Duncan had finally deigned to give her some attention.

He walked alongside her, saying nothing, but staring at her with an unnerving smile gracing his features. They continued into the room, and Caroline became further irritated to find that he had taken the seat to her right.

Said seat was usually occupied by Francis, and Caroline was now silently cursing her brother for spending the day riding with their grandfather instead.

"Dear Caroline," he finally began, "you must be positively ecstatic about your mother's engagement."

"You are being obvious." she replied, already tearing the bread roll for her soup into pieces.

"Now little one, I do not know why you are so convinced that I mean to tease you. After all, I have always been your greatest supporter."

"Name one example of you choosing to be kind to me rather than teasing." Caroline very much doubted he would be able to, but her sister apparently thought the subject too tedious.

"Do we have to listen to them bicker all lunch? I would have thought they have their fill it during the society affairs we attend."

"I did not think you noticed, Mina." Duncan said. "On every single occasion I have seen you this season you have been in the arms of Fawcett."

Caroline could not help but let out a giggle at the pink hue forming on her sister's cheeks.

"I can only assume you are referring to my dancing with Sir Ernest?" the younger girl defended herself. "I know better than to disgrace myself in public."

Caroline glanced at her mother and was unsurprised to see her face frozen in shock at Wilhelmina's words. She herself was trying not to grimace at her sister's lack of tact. No doubt Wilhelmina had not considered that her words bore an insult to their Mama.

"I have had the honour of dinner with your fiancé on many occasions since Harry wed his sister, cousin." Duncan turned away from Wilhelmina to address Anne, choosing to ignore the remark. Caroline had one reason to be grateful to the man it appeared. "Though I cannot say I know him well, he does leave a positive impression. I am certain he shall be a good husband for you."

As their mother warmly responded, Caroline took the opportunity to toss a piece of bread at her sister to attract the bemused girl's attention.

"What is wrong with you?" she mouthed, but it seemed to only confuse the girl even further.

Of course, Caroline also became confused, as her sister began mouthing words in return which she did not recognise at all. Perhaps her sister had secretly begun studying Russian in the hopes of impressing her beau?

Sending the younger girl one more befuddled glance, she returned her attention to the current discussion.

"I must confess," Duncan was saying, "I did corner Sutton for information on his friend, but the man had only glowing compliments to share."

"You would think they had been close friends for years." she sarcastically commented.

"Even so, I think the judgement of my cousin's husband is one we can rely on." her mother replied.

Duncan, on the other hand, returned to staring at Caroline, his eyes narrowing. She braced herself yet again for the onslaught.

This time she was not disappointed.

"Do you know who else had positive things to say of the man?" he started. "My younger brother."

Caroline almost laughed at his unoriginality. Harry had always been the go-to subject for Duncan's teasing. One day he would find another way to rile her up.

"In that case, then I imagine that the duke is far better than I had initially thought." she responded. "For we all know that Harry is an excellent judge of character."

"Naturally. It is why he always ran away from you as a child."

"That is interesting, I only remember him running to my defence on the occasions when you decided to subject me to yet another one of your teasing's." Caroline took a sip of her water before continuing. "It is fascinating how our memories of the past differ, is it not?"

"Especially when one is looking at it through rose-tinted glasses, I think."

"And I think that when one is indulging oneself in rakish behaviour, they are no doubt addling their mind somewhat and are so unable to remember things correctly."

"I shall keep that in mind when I write my next book." He smiled at her retort, a most unintended response.

"What are you writing about this time, Duncan?" Anne asked.

"The trials of aging." Caroline hastily said before the man could respond.

"Caroline." her mother uttered in warning.

"Aging, history, what is the difference?" Duncan dismissively responded.

"I just thought that, as our cousin is getting on in age, that his works might become self-reflective."

"Is five and twenty considered old now?" Wilhelmina asked, her expression still of confusion.

"If my works are reflective of my own state of mind, I wonder what the subject of Eleanor of Aquitaine means." Duncan pondered, not rising to Caroline's bait.

"I can think of one thing it might mean." her sister grinned, shocking the rest of the table.

"Wilhelmina Morton!" their mother exclaimed. "What on earth are you suggesting?"

The girl looked pleadingly about the table for assistance. As her eyes lingered on Caroline's, she received an enquiring face in return.

Caroline was interested in seeing what her sister would say. Especially if it meant that she had been sneakily learning about things a young lady had no right to know about. And not told her!

"Well..........I often overhear things said about Duncan." she timidly whispered. Duncan's face was positively dancing with glee now.

"Oh? What is said about me now?" his voice then dropped. "Is it scandalous?"

She did her best to hide it, but a small smile fell across Caroline's lips at how joyful he was. It appeared that his manner relaxed her sister as well.

"I do not think it is anything new." she giggled out. "Just that you prefer the company of married women."

"WILHELMINA!"

"I do not know what that means, Mama! Just that people say it."

"What on earth does this have to do with Eleanor of Aquitaine?" Caroline asked, more confused than ever. Wilhelmina shook her head at her sister in confusion.

"She was married twice."

Caroline did not understand it at all. The way her sister reacted in surprise to Duncan's head falling back in laughter made her think that she did not understand it entirely either.

"Now that is a thought." Duncan wickedly replied.

Caroline now had a new reason to wish to marry: To finally understand what everyone was talking about!

Chapter Four

"Sugar?"

Caroline's mind had wandered as the Duchess of Gloucester had been pouring her tea. Quickly nodding, she smiled and gave her thanks as the cup was handed to her.

"Now, Caroline dear," Cora began, "you must be honest with me."

Confused, she nodded at the expectant woman, who then smiled softly at her.

"I understand that a great deal of change has been thrust at your feet, I hope it is not causing you anguish."

"Why should I feel anguished?"

"I imagine with your stepmother becoming engaged, and your sister no doubt also heading in that general direction, you must feel a little lost. I certainly know I would be."

It suddenly made sense to Caroline why she had been invited to take tea with her great-aunt. She also now understood as to why the invitation had not been extended to her mother and sister. The latter of which had been particularly put out by the snub.

"I can assure you, Aunt Cora," Caroline answered, "as sudden and unexpected as it has all been, it is not the sort of thing that I shall struggle over for long."

Her aunt did not appear to believe her, so Caroline continued.

"Truly, when I think of how difficult it was when Papa died, this does not compare."

Nor to learning your youngest son had wed.

Of course, Caroline did not say that part aloud. Nonetheless, the Duchess seemed to have been placated by her words, as her shoulders relaxed somewhat.

"Nonetheless," she said, "should you ever need to escape for a while, you are more than welcome to visit with us."

"Thank you, Aunt. Though I am determined to approach matters in a more mature manner than I might be capable of, I shall resolve to keep your offer in mind."

"Please do. I must confess, I have found it odd having only my husband here for company. I am forever hosting to keep myself occupied."

Caroline smiled politely, uncertain if she should laugh or not. Luckily, the Duchess quickly changed the topic.

"Have you been enjoying your first season? You have waited so long for it."

"I must confess," she responded, "it is not entirely as I imagined, but I find it exciting nonetheless."

"I had worried that you and your sister would have expectations so high that they could not possibly be met."

If Caroline was honest about what she had expected her first season to be like, she would say that it bore no resemblance to reality. Primarily because of the gentleman she imagined courting her.

"In my girlish imagination, I did think I would be swept off my feet by a handsome gentleman." She smiled at the foolishness of the notion.

"I think we all expect it to be that way. Thus far, I have not encountered a lady who has found it to be reality."

"You clearly have not discussed this with my sister, then." Cora's eyes widened at that.

"Ah, yes. Sir Ernest. I did not think it wise to discuss *that* particular gentleman given our history."

Caroline thought that might be a chance at gaining some useful knowledge. She knew that he and Connie had been engaged before she married the Earl, and that it ended scandalously. But no one would tell her why.

"Mina and I have asked Mama about it countless times, but she never gives us an answer. All we get is *you shall know when you wed.* Whatever that means."

The corners of Cora's mouth lifted in amusement at her obviousness.

"I think the less people who know of why my daughter's engagement ended, the better."

"Why do I imagine it was similar to how Mama's engagement began?"

The Duchess did not answer, she simply lifted her teacup and took a few sips.

Yes, Caroline was definitely not going to get any answers until she was married. An event that was highly unlikely to happen anytime soon.

"Have there been any young gentlemen who have taken your fancy?" Cora asked, tactfully changing the subject.

Caroline sighed. "They are all perfectly nice."

"That is a no, then."

"Unfortunately." she confirmed. "I just find that they all sort of blend together. Unless I am speaking to one of them directly, I find I can often not tell them apart. And even then, I struggle to remember anything more than their name."

"I doubt they are all bad."

"You could ask me about any one of them and I would probably give you the same answer. There is nothing at all that sets each one apart from the others."

"I understand it may be frustrating," the Duchess set her teacup down as she spoke, "but you must be careful not to be too dismissive of them."

"That is easier said than done." Caroline balked.

"Perhaps, but it would do you no good to garner a reputation amongst the men. Would you not rather have many similar suitors than none at all?"

"I know. I find myself suppressing all my instincts whenever in society." A devious smile then crossed her face. "I have dropped a few hints, though, that I shall be more amenable to wed in the next season. That should give me enough time to whittle them down to the more agreeable gentlemen."

The Duchess narrowed her gaze upon the younger girl.

"Why next season?" she asked.

"Between Mama and Wilhelmina, I should imagine that our time will be taken up with weddings, and a break should do us all the world of good."

"I would be surprised if many men agree to your terms."

"I would be more surprised if they did not." Caroline replied. "The expectation of this oversized dowry Mama's intended is offering is motivation enough for them."

"Perhaps the time to whittle them down is...." Cora's voice trailed off as her eyes flicked towards the drawing room doorway followed by the appearance of a beaming smile. "Harry!"

Caroline froze at the exclamation. She had not seen the man who held her heart for years and was not prepared at all to face him now.

As the Duchess stood to greet her youngest son, Caroline took a deep breath, fixed a smile upon her face and turned in her chair to face him.

Outwardly, she maintained a warm and steady composure. Inwardly, however, her heart was fluttering, and her mind was consumed by how the man stood before her was even more handsome than before.

His features appeared more chiselled with age, but his perfect emerald eyes were still full of youthful vitality. Though he walked with a slight limp, it did not take away from his commanding presence and she thought he appeared rather majestic with his cane.

Willing her cheeks not to redden, she maintained a sense of decorum as he bent down to kiss her cheek in greeting before lowering himself into the seat beside hers. How she managed that, she did not know, as her heart practically leapt out of her chest at the contact of his mouth on her cheek.

"Miss Caroline," he said, his voice huskier than she remembered, "you are very lucky that I am in a good mood today, otherwise I would scold you for stealing my seat."

Caroline almost jumped into the air in her eagerness to vacate the armchair.

"Stop teasing, Henry." his mother ordered as she began piling biscuits onto a plate for him. "Ignore him, Caroline, he is only after the footstool."

Lowering herself back into the chair, Caroline looked down and saw the item in question to the left. Looking up to her right, she saw Harry grinning as he tapped his left leg with his cane.

Hearing the muffled sound of wood hitting wood, she leant down a little too eagerly to fetch the stool for him. He waved off her attempt to arrange it for him, causing Caroline to fill up with pride at how well he had accustomed himself to living with his injury.

"I do hope it does not cause you much pain, Captain." she said in earnest.

"Half the time, I forget it is missing." he replied. "And what is this 'Captain' business? Now that we are both grown, Have I ceased to be Harry?"

"Of course not," Caroline blushed, "I should wish to call you by the rank at least once, though. You are my war hero cousin, after all."

Rather than take it as a compliment, a queer look came upon Harry's face, and Caroline became cross with herself for upsetting him.

"Did you hear that, Mama?" he suddenly said, grinning. "I am a war hero! I must remember that whenever I want something from Eliza."

Though Caroline was relieved he had not taken offense, her heart sank at the reminder that the man she loved was so lost to her.

"Whatever you get from Eliza you no doubt deserve." Cora said to her son, who simply shrugged.

"I must find some way of reminding her of the dashing young man she fell for, being cooped up in the house with two small children is not exactly making her agreeable."

"It most certainly is not if her husband goes off making surprise visits and leaving her there, either." his mother scolded.

Caroline, however, did not agree with her sentiment. To be able to spend her days at home as Harry's wife, taking care of their children and loving him would be all she wanted. If Elizabeth Ainsworth was not thrilled with that arrangement, then she was the biggest fool in all of England.

"Now, now," Harry defended himself, "she often visits Connie or her mother and sisters for tea. In fact, she is with her eldest sister now, she took the children so they could play with their cousins."

"Oh, that is a shame." the Duchess cooed. "I would have loved to see her and the little ones."

No, it is not!

"You saw them two days ago!" her son exclaimed, directing a knowing smile Caroline's way, reminding her to ensure the scowl on her mind did not form on her face.

"That is never enough for a grandmother."

"Speaking of grandmothers," Harry turned to face Caroline fully now, "when are you going to make my cousin one?"

"Harry!"

Caroline's mouth dropped at his brazenness, unable to say anything for a moment. She soon recovered, though, and burst into laughter.

"I think you should ask my sister that instead, Harry, she is the one who we expect to be wed by the end of the season."

"Why not you?" he asked. "Surely the men of the ton are not foolish enough to fail to see the greatest prize in London before all of them?"

"I have suitors, but I find none of them to be good enough."

And they are not you.

Understanding crossed his features, and he nodded in agreement.

"Quite right. You should not settle for any less than you deserve!" he declared. "Which, in your case, is the best."

I love you.

Caroline could barely remember anything said for the rest of the visit. All she could think about was the way he spoke to her.

Every other sentence he was full of praise, and she became certain that he was looking at her with the same love in his eyes that she bore for him.

Oh, how utterly wretched it was, Caroline thought, that such love could not be realised.

When it was time for Caroline to return home, Harry told his mother that he should do the same, and so escorted her directly to her carriage.

Taking her hand from its place in the crook of his arm, he pressed a soft kiss to it, causing her heart to flutter once more.

"I am so glad we can be friends, Miss Caroline." he said as he bid his goodbye.

From her seat in the carriage, Caroline stared at him until he was no longer in view. She wanted to weep at how she was not able to openly show the love she felt for him.

Something about his manner, though, and the way he looked and spoke to her, told Caroline that he knew what was in her heart. Not only that, but that he felt the same.

The laws of society made it so that they could never be together as they wished, but somehow, she knew that one day, whether tomorrow or years from now, Harry Wexford was going to kiss her.

And they would be together, society be damned!

Chapter Five

The day had finally arrived.

Caroline had made a handful of half-hearted attempts to stop it, but her efforts had proven to be as futile as she had expected.

She watched as her beloved Mama stood before the vicar and joined her in marriage to the Duke of Bristol. Though she was loathe to admit it, Caroline was beginning to like the man.

Any attempts to replace her father, however, would result in him meeting her wrath.

She could not deny they were a handsome pair. No doubt their children would be perfect, at least visually. That thought caused a minor twinge in Caroline's heart. She would love any children Anne had as though they did share blood, but she could not help but feel a little sad at the thought of them looking to another man as their father.

The wedding breakfast was to be held at her new home. She bundled into a carriage with her sister, brother, and grandparents and almost laughed at how stilted the atmosphere was for the short journey.

No one spoke to acknowledge it, but it was as though a feeling of the inevitable having happened, all the while, they had all somewhat denied the thought of it actually happening until the deed was done.

She had visited the house briefly before, but now, stood in the large entrance hall, Caroline fully took in the grand interior. At least that distracted her from the company.

She refrained specifically from looking in the direction of the staircase as, gathered just to its left were her new stepfather's three sisters, accompanied by the husbands of the two married women.

It was of no use to see them together, for Caroline would simply burn with more jealousy than she already had at Eliza Ainsworth who, during the single glance in that direction Caroline had allowed herself, was stood comfortably with her husband's hand resting on her waist.

It would do no good for Harry to see how much it tormented her!

"Would you like some advice?" a deep voice suddenly whispered in her ear, causing her to release a small squeak.

Turning, Caroline was totally unsurprised to find Duncan grinning down at her.

"Oh, I should have known it was you."

"You make it sound as though my whispering in your ear is a common occurrence."

"It happens far too much for my liking."

"I have only done it once!"

"And that is more than enough." She could not help it, but his smile was infectious, and Caroline found herself shaking her head, annoyed at how amused and at ease he was making her.

"You did not answer my question, you know." Duncan said.

"What question?"

"I asked you if you would like some advice?" Caroline rolled her eyes at him.

"I never wish for your advice, Duncan, and yet I get it all the same."

"Perhaps my question should be would you like to heed my advice then?"

"Then you should finally give me advice that is useful."

His mouth tightened at that. Caroline was unsure if it meant that he was trying to hide his amusement or if he was irritated by her.

Besides his other irritable traits, she was most annoyed by how difficult he was to read sometimes.

Letting out an exaggerated sigh, she narrowed her eyes at him.

"What is this unsolicited advice then?"

"I do not feel like giving it now. You are far too ungrateful." he answered lazily, looking about the room instead of at her.

"Good, then we both get what we want."

"Do we?" Caroline was unnerved by his question.

"What is that supposed to mean?"

"Oh, nothing." he responded before changing the subject. "I suppose now that you and your sister are the most eligible maidens in society, I should expect your engagement announcement very soon."

"I doubt that." Caroline laughed. "Besides, I do not think that you would ever learn of it from an announcement. Knowing my luck, you would be there when it happened."

"That is a delicious thought." Duncan's smile spread wider. "But why should you ever think I would be there?"

She knew he was playing the fool, as the man knew well enough how he always found himself there at the most opportune moments, but she played along, nonetheless.

"Because, my least favourite cousin, you seem to make it your mission to hunt me out for your teasing pleasure. I would not be surprised to find you there on my wedding night, ready to make some barb at me and my new husband."

Of course, Duncan Wexford would be the only person she knew that would not find the comment scandalous.

"I can just imagine it now." he said wistfully. "*Not like that......put it there......you are doing it wrong.*"

Caroline's eyes lit up at the last part.

"And what way should it be done, dearest Duncan?"

It almost worked. Duncan's mouth briefly opened to answer her, but it quickly shut again, and he directed at her a disapproving look.

"You know I shall go to my grave before I ever tell you." His face lightened then. "In any case, you are precisely the sort of girl who would choose to marry someone who has no clue what to do. So, there is no point in trying to tell you, for you would just end up disappointed."

A wicked thought crossed Caroline's mind. She made her expression appear as innocent as possible as she gazed up at him.

"Perhaps instead of the husband, it should be you teaching me instead, then."

His eyes widened in shock at her brazen suggestion, then darkened and, for a moment, Caroline quivered under the intensity of his gaze.

What the devil is the chit playing at?

Duncan knew the conversation was veering into dangerous territory. He felt comfortable playing along at first, as the only people who surrounded them were family or those they could trust.

If you had told him five years ago that he would count the Ainsworth family of all people in that group, he would have scoffed and then laughingly repeated the jest to anyone who could listen for the next several days.

In any case, he was only playing along with Caroline as long as it did not go too far.

It had gone too far!

He stared down at her, refusing to let any sort of amusement appear on his face.

"Never ever make a suggestion like that again, Caroline Morton!" he scolded.

She simply gazed up at him, fluttering her eyelashes in faux innocence but Duncan knew that behind those doe eyes lurked a devious little wench.

"What sort of a suggestion?" she asked.

"You know perfectly well what you said."

"Now Duncan, dear," her voice was still light and airy as she played dumb, "as an innocent maiden, how can I possibly know what I was suggesting?"

He was surprised when a growl threatened to come out of his mouth. Yes, Caroline was a maiden and innocent, but she knew when she was crossing the line, even if she did not know precisely what that line entailed.

She still gazed up at him, waiting for an answer but she would not get one. Not now that there were images flashing across his mind of other ways that she could be looking up at him.

In all of the images, the pair of them were in varying stages of undress, and his mouth suddenly felt rather parched.

Why did she have to go and put that train of thought in his mind?

"I understand that our friendship may allow us to be more comfortable with one another than others," he said, wishing to put an end to her insanity, "and my reputation may give the impression that you may freely speak to you, but rest assured, Caroline, you can never say a thing like that to me again."

Her face contorted into a frown at that.

"Duncan......"

"Dear god, Caroline!" he interrupted, refusing to allow her to even try to defend herself. "What if someone heard you? Have you no consideration for your mother or sister?"

Her eyes widened in shock. He doubted he had ever been so serious with her.

Duncan had little interest in hearing any more. Inclining his head to her, he turned on his heel and moved to join his father and uncle.

Swiping a glass of champagne from a passing tray, he downed it in one go. He could hear the words leave the mouths of the men in front of him, but Duncan could make no sense of them. All he could think of were the words that had emerged from the girl's lips.

Lips he had never thought of before, but now he thought that they were perfect for performing scandalous acts upon his person.

Wonderful, he rued, now whenever he thought of the girl, he would be thinking of her in all sorts of positions.

As soon as this blasted breakfast was over, Duncan decided, he was going to seek out a woman for his bed. A woman who was the furthest thing from pure, little, Caroline Morton, who would serve as a reminder of why he only sought after experienced women.

Yes, he was only thinking of Caroline now because she had put the thought of herself in his mind, and the only women currently around were relatives, and thus unable to distract him from the thought of the brunette.

He needed a real woman!

The day continued on, and he did his utmost to avoid Caroline, though he could not resist throwing a handful of looks her way. As he turned back after one of these looks, he found his older brother smirking at him.

"What?" Duncan demanded,

"Why do you keep looking at Caroline?"

"Material to tease her with." He kept his voice uncaring, to not give a hint of the explicit thoughts in his head.

"Your eyes keep glancing to her bosom, even you would not tease her about that."

"I thought I was a rake who knew no boundaries."

"So, you do not deny looking at her chest?"

"Look, I am friends with Caroline. Caroline is a woman with all the pertaining parts and sometimes, as a man, I find myself observing those womanly features."

Duncan was flabbergasted that this conversation was happening. Even worse was how amused his brother appeared to be at it.

"I cannot help but notice that you always seek her out when she is within somewhat close proximity."

"Of course I will!" Duncan exclaimed. "The girl is the easiest person to tease. How can you expect me to resist the urge to do so?"

Matt's expression began to turn from amused to serious and he spoke his next words slowly, as though he was carefully considering each word.

"Are you certain that it is only that? As it has looked a little different to some of us."

"My behaviour towards Caroline has not changed one bit since we were children. It is most definitely *only that*."

His brother nodded his head slowly. "Just be careful, will you. If the ones who already know of the dynamic the two of you share are getting certain impressions, one can only imagine what those who do not know of it think."

Duncan was unable to formulate a response, as Matt was immediately called away by his wife. He simply stared at the older man's retreating form, gobsmacked over the conversation that had just occurred.

Thinking over what his brother said, Duncan realised he would indeed have to stay away from Caroline. At least for a while. This combined with the suggestions that his own reputation could compromise her own was too great to ignore.

He was now feeling rather put out by it all, having to give up the perfect victim for his teasing.

Caroline rarely took major offence to his words, gave as good as she got and formulated the perfect expressions of horror and embarrassment at his words.

Not only that, but she was in the prime time for his teasing. Her first season! Having all sorts of young men thrust themselves at her.

Duncan was going to miss out on some of the best fun of his life!

Chapter Six

In the most unsurprising development, barely a week after their mother had wed, Sir Ernest Fawcett got down on one knee and asked Wilhelmina to marry him.

Caroline heard the squeal from the other end of the house.

In the two weeks that had passed since that occasion, the chaos that had reigned in the preparations for Anne's wedding returned. This time, however, it seemed to have doubled, for Liam had kindly agreed to host an engagement ball for the couple.

It was only fitting that the event echoed Caroline's experiences in society of the past few weeks, and thus, she was constantly surrounded by suitors. The number of which had seemingly tripled since the wedding.

Surprisingly, Liam had assisted in scaring away the more undesirable ones, for which she was thankful, but that did not stop the majority of them.

Caroline also found it unexpected that the most irritating thing was not the tediousness of the men that she had come to expect. Instead, she was horrified to realise that her dance card had been filled entirely. Not one moment of the ball from the opening waltz would be free for her and, by the end of the fifth dance, her feet were already suffering from it all.

With a smile plastered on her face, she danced waltzes, quadrilles, cotillions and other dances she could not remember. She made polite enquiries to each of her partners, answered their own, determined that they would not make a good match, and gave noncommittal answers to their more serious suggestions.

Remembering the Duchess' advice, Caroline knew that it would do her prospects no good to give the impression that she was unamiable to wed. Just as she had promised, she put out the suggestion that she would prefer to wait until the next season to marry.

Just as she expected with her new dowry and connections, the mass of suitors showed no sign of being put off by her decision, and she had received much praise for her kindness on reducing the amount of stress for her mother.

After her seventh dance, Caroline waited by the side of the dance floor for her next partner to join her, but he simply did not appear.

Looking about the crowd for the black hair of Mr Horton…. or was he red haired Caroline wondered……she could not see him anywhere.

Realising she had a much-needed reprieve, she quickly absconded from the ballroom. She snuck out to the gardens, where there were several hiding spots that she had found over the past weeks.

There, she decided, Caroline would spend a moment savouring the quiet.

Finding a bench, she slipped off her slippers and began to massage her feet. For the next ball, she resolved, she would make sure to leave every fourth or fifth dance empty, so she could at least have a drink.

Allowing her eyes to drift shut, Caroline tuned out the sounds of revelry coming from the house and emptied her mind for a moment. Savouring the peace, she let out a deep breath.

A sudden shriek brought her out of her tranquil state. Her eyes snapping open, Caroline turned to her right, straining her ears for any other noises in the darkness.

She heard nothing.

Nonetheless, Caroline decided that the noise she had heard sounded like a lady in distress and lifted her skirts to tiptoe in that direction. If a gentleman thought to take advantage in her mother's house, he would find himself faced with a young lady out for vengeance.

Peering around each corner, she found nothing amiss. About to give up, she began to turn back the way she came when the sound of rustling reached Caroline's ears.

Frowning, she followed the noise and peered into a small gap between a stone way and a hedge walkway. Her hand immediately rose to cover her mouth as her eyes widened in shock and horror.

Leaning against the ivy-covered wall with her eyes shut and her mouth open, was Anne. She was breathing heavily and clutching at her dress.

Caroline's eyes drifted downwards and saw that it was not only the dress that Anne was clutching. Underneath her skirts, held in place by the woman's left hand, aligned with what the girl supposed was her mother's most private area, was a rather large lump.

This lump grew larger the lower down it went, until Caroline saw two legs sticking out from underneath. Two legs that were *not* her mother's.

No, they certainly belonged to a gentleman, most likely her new stepfather. But why on earth should he be kneeling underneath Anne's skirts?

And why would it be bringing about such a visceral reaction in her Mama?

Whatever it was, Caroline was certain it was to do with what went on in the marriage bed. Her cheeks began to flush upon hearing the small sounds of pleasure coming from her mother's mouth.

Realising how horrific it would be to be caught watching such a private moment between the newlyweds, she tiptoed away from the pair until she thought herself safely out of earshot to allow her to flee the gardens entirely. Stopping only to pick up her forgotten slippers, of course.

Caroline did not stop running until she reached the terrace that led back to the ballroom. Breathing erratically, she stumbled as she put her slippers back on.

Frantically fanning her face, she realised that she needed to escape somewhere to calm herself down for a moment. It would most certainly do her no good to immediately be swept up in a dance when she was still suffering from witnessing her mother in the throes of passion.

Scanning her eyes across the building, she spotted the door that led to her Mama's study, and hurried over to it, praying it had not been locked yet.

Turning the handle, Caroline breathed a sigh of relief to find the door click open. She rushed into the room, shut the door behind her, and practically fell into the chair behind the desk. Her head fell into her hands as she stared at the dark wood of the desk.

Trying to catch her breath, Caroline found herself muttering all sorts of encouragements under her breath. The primary one, of course, being "calm down."

Gradually, her breathing began to steady, and her heart began to stop threatening to burst out of her chest.

Looking up at last, she shrieked, and her heart resumed its pounding as she saw Duncan staring at her with interest from an armchair beside the fireplace. The only light came from the moonlight through the doors to the terrace, making half his face shrouded in darkness, which only served to further unnerve her.

"Why is it," she sputtered in her speech, "that whenever I find myself in distress, you appear?"

"I was here first." came the reply.

"Why did you not say anything?"

He shifted awkwardly, staring down at some drink he had in his hand. "You looked like you had everything under control."

Leaning back in her seat, Caroline crossed her arms, observing her mother's cousin through narrowed eyes.

"Where have you been these past weeks?" she asked.

"What do you mean?"

"I have attended two balls, five exhibits, three garden parties and one race since my mother's wedding, and you have been nowhere to be found. Why is that?"

His eyes flitted about the room, refusing to meet her own.

"What I do with my time is of no importance to you, Caroline Morton. Believe it or not, I do not have to spend every minute with you."

Caroline's cheeks reddened at the chastisement.

"I simply find it odd that you went from being a constant nuisance to completely absent. I shall not bother asking after you again."

He nodded in acknowledgement. Still feeling rather flustered, Caroline fanned herself with her hand. Aside from the horror of what she had witnessed, she had a strange feeling that was affecting her most private parts. A feeling of both excitement and anticipation that she had no clue as to how to handle.

"What happened?" Duncan asked, his voice quizzical. Caroline's hand froze in front of her face, so she slowly lowered it to rest with the other on her lap.

"Whatever do you mean?" she tried to keep her voice light.

He rose out of his seat to move to the front of the desk. With his palms resting over the surface, he leaned over and stared intently at her.

Caroline kept her eyes on his own as she tried to hide how out of sorts she was. No doubt if she revealed any of what had passed to Duncan, she would suffer once he deigned to resume his teasing enterprise.

"Your face is flustered," he said bluntly, "and your eyes are like saucers."

He continued to study her, much to Caroline's annoyance. Feeling the need to escape the room, she opened her mouth to excuse herself. She was stopped, however, when a flicker of realisation crossed his eyes and they widened in horror.

"Caroline Morton, you tell me what has happened right this moment!" he ordered.

"I was feeling overwhelmed, so I went for a walk to calm myself." She supposed it was technically the truth. "Now, if you will excuse me, I am taken for the next dance."

Standing and moving about the desk, she thought she was going to escape without further question. That is, until a pair of hands suddenly clasped her waist.

With ease, Duncan turned her in his arms to face him and pulled her against him. The action did nothing to soothe the mysterious feeling traipsing through Caroline's body as she had never been so close to a man before. Now she could feel every inch of him.

"Duncan!" she exclaimed.

"This is serious, Caroline." She had never seen his eyes so wild. "If something has happened, you must say so. Nothing is more important than your honour."

"The only thing threatening my honour at this moment is you." she protested, pushing her hands against his chest. Caroline tried to ignore the fact that her body was only resisting his hold half-heartedly.

"Give me the cad's name and I will ensure he weds you."

"What?" Caroline was growing desperate. "I promise no one has compromised me, Duncan."

He was silently staring at her again, his eyes searching her face for proof that she was telling the truth. She gazed back at him, trying to wordlessly alleviate the man's fears.

After a moment, she began to feel the strangest thing. Duncan had never exactly shared the athletic frame of his brothers, so Caroline was not particularly surprised to find that his body was a little soft when pressed against hers.

What did surprise her, was a sudden hardness pressing against her stomach. Confused she glanced down but in the dim light could not make out what it was.

Looking back up, she saw that his face had darkened, and looked a little pained.

"Duncan," she said, "what is that?"

He did not answer her. Instead, hearing her voice made his eyes fall to gaze at her lips. Caroline felt his hands, resting on the small of her back, begin to lightly press her closer to him and an anguished groan rumbled from his mouth.

Why was her breathing suddenly so heavy?

Caroline had no clue what was going on, but she was starting to feel as though this was connected to what she had seen in the gardens.

His eyes still focused upon her mouth; Duncan's head began to slowly lean down towards hers. If Caroline did not know any better, she would have thought that Duncan was about to kiss her.

Whatever he was going to do, he was jolted out of it by the loud laughter of unknown gentlemen passing by the study door.

Caroline stumbled in surprise as he quickly pushed her away. She only caught one glimpse of his face before he ran out of the room, but she thought it seemed rather horrified.

Taking a moment to regather her wits, Caroline fell into the chair the man had occupied not a few moments ago. Picking up his abandoned glass, she sniffed the amber liquid and then drained the whole thing in one mouthful.

Coughing at the bitter taste, she felt a little better at the warmth she felt in her stomach. She just wished it could help the confusion over all that had just happened.

And the strange feeling she still had in her most private of places.

Chapter Seven

Duncan thought he was doing a good job. Against his better nature, he had kept away from society affairs to ensure that he could get Caroline out of his mind.

Several liaisons with mature, knowledgeable women had seemed to do the trick but then one encounter had gone and ruined all his hard work.

In fact, it might have made it worse! It was clear as day that the girl had been aroused. Even more beguiling was that she was obviously so innocent that she had no idea what she was feeling. Duncan had wanted nothing more than to thoroughly corrupt her in that study.

Where would that lead him though? He might be a rake. He might be a cad. But he possessed at least a little sense of honour. Duncan would have married her immediately and been stuck with the girl as the novelty wore off.

Thus, he had run away like a coward. He left the ball, returned to his bachelor lodgings, and furiously beat his cock until he reached an unsatisfactory release. All the while, he thought of her face staring up at him when he held her in his arms.

Her cheeks were charmingly flushed, her eyes glazed over in a mix of arousal and confusion, she had pressed herself against him.

Duncan then spent the night dreaming of what would have happened had he given in to his desires. When he woke in the morning, he found himself in sweaty tangled bedsheets. The first time he had ever done so without the company of a woman.

With a groan, he took a cold bath and readied for the day. He cursed at his valet upon being reminded that he agreed to meet with his brothers at their club that morning.

Keeping his plans, he arrived at White's early, settled into a seat, ordered a glass of brandy and read the paper as he waited.

"Am I still asleep? Either that or my lack of sleep is making me hallucinate."

Duncan peered up from his paper to find his brother staring down at him, his face contorted in befuddlement.

"Good day to you too."

Matt moved to sit opposite him, examining Duncan in the most peculiar manner. Duncan gave him a pointed look to express his annoyance at the examination.

"You are early." The older man finally said.

"So?"

"You are never early. You are always the last to arrive." His brother's eyes then widened in horror. "Dear God! You are dying, are you not?"

Duncan smothered a grin at how his brother's mind was reaching.

"How long have you known?" Matt continued. "For Christ sake's man, I told you that it would not hurt to indulge yourself a little less."

"Indulge myself in what, may I ask? Women? Drink? Food?"

"Whichever one is relevant."

"Fortunately for me, none of them are." Duncan reassured. "As far as I am aware, my death is not imminent."

He was somewhat touched at how Matt let out a relieved breath. The man still appeared confused, though.

"Why are you early then?"

"Can I not be early every so often?"

"I have never, in my life, ever known you to be early." His brother countered. "You detest not getting enough sleep and because there is normally a woman in your bed, you end up sleeping late."

"I am not that bad!"

"I did not expect you for at least another hour."

"Why is Duncan here already?"

The men turned to find their youngest brother staring at them, the same dumbfounded expression on his face as Matt.

"Why is it so shocking that I should arrive first for once?" Duncan exclaimed.

"Because you never are." Harry answered as he took the chair between his brothers. "Something must have happened. Good God, are you ill?"

"I already asked. He claims he is not, but I still maintain something is wrong."

A devilish smile appeared on his younger brother's face. "Did you leave a woman unsatisfied for the first time?"

"That is not a possibility." Duncan denied, though his mind drifted back to the memory of Caroline in the study. "I leave that to the pair of you."

"I can assure you; I have no trouble in that department." Matt said.

"As can I."

"I doubt your wives would agree."

"We have one woman each to master the art of pleasure for, you have numerous." Harry replied. "I think statistically, you are more likely to get it wrong one day."

"And I think that you are more likely to get lazy one day."

Harry looked far too smug in response, Duncan thought, whilst Matt simply rolled his eyes. He waited as they ordered their own drinks, using the time to think up more cutting remarks for the two irritants.

"What is going on with you, then?" Matt asked, looking particularly serious.

Duncan opened his mouth to reply with one of his barbs. But his brother appeared to see the remark coming and pointed his finger at him.

"I want a serious answer, Dunc. I already learnt my lesson from not seeing past this one's light-hearted demeanour."

Duncan sighed, if Matt was using how Harry hid his misery over his feelings for Eliza before their marriage, he would not let it go.

"I did not sleep well, that is all." He gave them that but had no intention of giving the reason for his sleep troubles.

"That is not like you." Harry commented.

"I have been stuck on some wording for my book," Duncan lied, "it has been distracting."

"Perhaps we can help." Matt suggested, earning himself a disbelieving look from his brother. "It was just a suggestion." He shrugged in response.

"My ego would not allow it. Just the thought of it being mentioned at the dinner table fills me with dread."

"I would not just want it mentioned then," Harry grinned, "I should expect to be named co-author."

"If Harry is being credited, then so will I be."

"Wonderful," Duncan sarcastically replied, *"The Life and Times of Eleanor of Aquitaine by the Wexford Brothers."*

"Has a certain charm to it." Harry nodded. "Of course, I do not believe that your book is why you are having trouble sleeping but if you do not wish to reveal it, I shall use other means to uncover the truth."

"What means?"

Duncan would like to know as well. He watched suspiciously as his younger brother covered his mouth and seemed to be mouthing something to his elder one. Matt, in response, nodded his head, impressed at whatever Harry had suggested.

The pair turned back to him with knowing looks on their faces. Irritated, Duncan decided to not give them the satisfaction and decided to change the subject.

"How is mourning, Harry? Are you having fun?"

Harry let out a groan. "We have decided that we will begin our return to society at Wilhelmina's wedding, Lord knows we need it."

"I would have thought a couple so in love as yourselves would enjoy having to lock themselves up together."

"We are not prisoners in our own home, Duncan, we can leave the house. We simply miss the social life of the season."

"I would have thought you would have relished in the excuse of staying away." Matt contributed.

"How so?"

"Just the thought of a certain lovesick maiden following you around amuses me."

Duncan had to suppress a groan at the thought. He needed to forget about her, not be reminded at every turn. Harry, on the other hand, simply stared at their brother in confusion.

"Who on earth are you speaking of?"

"A certain brunette sister of the bride." Matt lifted his eyebrows a few times in teasing.

"Caroline?" Harry still sounded bemused. "Surely, you do not think she still harbours that little infatuation from years ago?"

"You do not?" Duncan asked in disbelief.

"We have gone so long without speaking that she must have forgotten about me." Harry answered. "In any case, I ran into her when visiting Mama a little while ago, and she showed no signs of that little crush."

"When was this? She never mentioned it." Duncan said a little too hastily, earning an intrigued look from Matt.

Harry, luckily, remained oblivious and merely responded that it must be further proof that her feelings had been left in the past.

"I suppose that even if her infatuation with Harry does still linger," Matt said, "she is too distracted by her numerous suitors to do anything about it. Did you see her at the ball last night?"

Duncan coughed out some noncommittal answer that he had but did not reveal exactly how closely he had seen her.

"Aside from what I think was three dances," Matt continued, "she was constantly occupied on the dancefloor. I think you would have to join a waiting list to get the chance to see her, little brother."

"Is that so?" Harry's mouth pursed with interest. "Who would have thought that bratty little Caroline would be so popular?"

"She is not a brat, she is spirited." Duncan came to her defence. "Besides, her new stepfather is wealthy and well connected. She would attract a great deal of attention even if she were not so pretty to look at."

He winced the moment the last part left his mouth. One look at his brother's confirmed that he had said too much. Matt had a knowing look on his face whilst Harry was practically salivating at the entertainment potential.

"You think she is pretty to look at?" Matt asked.

"Objectively, yes. I am not blind Matthew!" Duncan protested. "Just because a person is of no interest to me, it does not mean that I cannot see with my own eyes if they are attractive or not."

"But you said *so pretty*. That phrasing is a tad more involved; do you not think?"

"In the context of my point it is understandable and no indication that I may possess an interest."

"Perhaps, but why should you not possess an interest?"

Duncan was incredulous at his older brother.

"Do you really need to ask that?" he exclaimed. "I have no desire to wed and only wish to have an older, experienced woman in my bed. Caroline does not match with any of those points. Not to mention the fact that this is *Caroline* we are discussing."

"Hmmm." Matt only responded.

Wondering why his youngest brother had not stuck his oar in yet, Duncan turned to him. Harry still had a devilish smile on his face, but behind his eyes, Duncan could see the cogs turning.

"Well?" He asked, already exasperated.

"It just makes sense." Harry carefully replied.

"What does?"

"You and Caroline. I had never thought of it before but now that I think about it, the pair of you are extraordinarily well matched."

"You are being ridiculous." Duncan replied.

"Come along man, she answers back to your barbs with ease. Name another woman who does that."

"Easily. Connie, Jane, Eliza, should I go on?"

Harry gave him an annoyed look.

"Name one that does not have to put up with you due to a familial connection."

"That already excludes Caroline." Duncan petulantly said.

"If you wish to be pedantic." Matt contributed.

"Even so," Harry continued without acknowledging his brother's point, "your eyes light up with just a mention of the girl."

"Harry, my eyes light up with just a mention of lemon cakes."

"You have just proven my point! You love lemon cakes."

"For god's sake." Duncan spat out, harshly opening the paper again. "If you two are going to keep like this, I will just ignore you."

Opening the pages, his brothers were now concealed from his view, but he still heard their sniggers.

"I would wager they will be engaged by the end of the season," he heard Harry say, "especially as I shall make it my mission to help them reach that goal."

"No," Matt contested, "our brother is far too stubborn to just get engaged to her. He will suppress his feelings until she is about to wed another, and then get himself into such a jealous frenzy that he kidnaps her before the wedding."

"How much would you like to bet on that?"

Duncan blocked out the noises of his brothers negotiating the boon. He was frustrated at how quickly they were able to discern some of his feelings.

They would be disappointed, however. He had no intention of wedding Caroline. He simply lusted after her. This would go one of three ways, Duncan surmised.

One: He would get over his little fantasy of the innocent girl.

Two: He would not get over his fantasy, but nothing would happen in any case.

Three: He would not get over his fantasy. Caroline would wed one of her insipid little suitors, pop out a couple of children and grow bored with her life. He would then sweep in and take her as a lover.

He knew he should not, but Duncan prayed that the third way would be the course he would go on.

Chapter Eight

"...and so, I ask you all to raise a glass to the new Lady Fawcett."

Caroline raised her glass and mumbled along with the rest of the guests. Looking across the room, she watched her sister gaze adoringly at her new husband and could not help but beam at the sheer joy on Wilhelmina's face.

She wanted to approach her sister, but the bride was surrounded by dozens of well-wishers. Instead, Caroline wandered about the entrance hall of Ainsworth House.

Unlike her mother's wedding the month before, this was most certainly not a quiet affair. Anne and Liam had only hosted their immediate families. This time, it seemed that all of London had turned out for her sister's wedding breakfast.

Spotting a trio of her fellow debutantes, Caroline sidled over to them.

"Miss Morton," Ada Duchannes greeted her, "I was just saying how well the blush suits the new Lady Fawcett."

Caroline nodded in agreement. "Pink has always been Wilhelmina's colour."

"I imagine this must be bittersweet for you, seeing your younger sister so happy." Lady Esther Eliot added.

"Certainly not." came Caroline's protest. "I wish for nothing more than Wilhelmina's happiness. That she should find it first merely means that I can focus on finding my own without worrying about her."

"How sweet." Ada replied, her smile too sickly to be genuine.

"I doubt we shall have to wait for much longer to hear of your engagement announcement."

Caroline turned to face Miss Juliette Simpson, a cousin of her stepfather's, who was barely hiding her contempt.

"That is funny, I thought I had made it quite clear that I did not plan to wed until next season, to give the family a chance to rest after two weddings in a row. Are you not privy to common gossip, Miss Simpson?"

She blinked innocently at the girl, who's blue eyes darkened at the barb.

"I had heard," she responded, "but the constant line of suitors at every function gave me a different impression."

"Perhaps it is a testament to Miss Morton that she is able to keep such a flock of men interested in spite of that announcement."

Caroline gave Esther a smile in gratitude. She had always found the girl to be kind, and she hoped that a proposal was on the horizon for her.

"Well, now that we understand that I am not to wed soon, what of the rest of you?" Caroline could not help but feel a small sense of victory at the sheepish look on Juliette's face. As far as she was aware, no gentleman had kept a prolonged interest in the girl.

The two kinder girls had more luck, apparently, as Ada confessed to eavesdropping on a request for her hand whilst Esther shyly told that she had been visited several times by a young officer.

Caroline heartily congratulated the pair and listened attentively as they described their beaux with smitten expressions on their faces.

As they went on, however, Caroline felt a small pang of jealousy in her chest and wished she could find someone who could make her feel the same way.

Someone who had not gone and married another, that is.

After a while, she saw her mother waving at her, and Caroline excused herself to find out what Anne wanted.

"Oh, Caroline!" her Mama said in surprise. "I thought you were enjoying yourself with your fellow debs."

Caroline frowned in confusion and reminded her mother that she had waved her over.

"Oh, sorry darling, I was not waving at you." Caroline felt her cheeks redden in embarrassment over her error. Naturally, her mother noticed, and began spluttering on that she was glad it happened in an attempt to appease her daughter.

"Do not fret, Mama." Caroline reassured. "I was wanting an excuse to leave anyway."

"Really? I imagined that you were enjoying spending time with girls your own age."

"I do. It was more the topic of conversation that I wished to escape from."

Anne looked at her expectantly and Caroline knew that she would have to explain further.

"They were discussing their young men," she explained, "and I just felt a bit lonely listening to it."

Her mother gave a sympathetic smile and rubbed Caroline's arm lightly.

"Just wait." she said. "The perfect gentleman will appear out of nowhere and sweep you off your feet."

"Is Caroline getting married now?" The mother and daughter turned to find that Liam had joined them, offering both women drinks.

Caroline graciously took one of the glasses but had the distinct impression that he had originally gotten the drink for himself.

"Unfortunately, you shall be stuck with me indefinitely." she remarked.

"Wonderful." Liam remarked. "I had to console your crying Mama last night. I should not like to repeat the experience anytime soon."

"*Liam!*" Anne scolded in horror, making Caroline laugh. He merely shrugged.

"I should hope you did, Mama. If just to prove that we are not that bad to live with."

"I would never say that." Caroline gave her mother a disbelieving look causing Anne to laugh. "I would not say it seriously."

"I would." Liam joked. "The sooner I am rid of all of you, the better."

"You would find life very lonely without us there, stepfather dearest."

Liam exaggerated a pondering expression, then his features widened as if he had just discovered the answer to a long-kept mystery.

"Heirs and lots of them!" he remarked. "That shall soothe the loneliness when you have left us."

"Do I have a say in this?" Anne asked, winking at her daughter.

"Of course, my love." Liam pulled her closer and planted a kiss on her nose. "Top or bottom?"

"Liam!"

Anne slapped his chest in horror but could not hide her amusement as she began to blush. Caroline's eyes darted between the pair, unsure of what the comment meant.

She suddenly felt as though she was trespassing on a very private moment between the couple, and her mind quickly searched for an escape route.

Her mind did not provide it, however her eyes did. Several steps away, framed in Caroline's vision by the married pair's love-struck faces, was who at this moment she decided was her favourite cousin.

Excusing herself, Caroline began to make her way over to him. Duncan was engaged in an animated conversation and as he spoke, his head turned, and his eyes met her own.

A beaming smile crossed her features and she waved slightly to the man as she continued towards him. It took her by the utmost surprise, therefore, when he suddenly disappeared.

Searching the room, Caroline could find no trace of the man. She moved to stand beside a bust of some Ainsworth ancestor as she frowned in confusion.

This was all the confirmation she needed. Duncan was most certainly avoiding her. But why, Caroline asked herself. She was not aware of having said or done anything of particular rudeness.

Well, there was that one jest about the marriage bed, but that was a month ago. She had never known Duncan Wexford of all people to hold a grudge for so long. That was her job!

She remained so still and silent as she pondered her thoughts, that Caroline did not seem to have been spotted by a pair of young gentlemen stood on the other side of the bust.

She noticed them, though. How could one not when they were not exactly being quiet as they spoke. Especially when Caroline heard her own name being mentioned.

"What do you think?" she heard a deep voice ask. "How long until Miss Morton gives in and allows herself to be courted seriously?"

Caroline found herself unconsciously pressing her back against the wall, as though it would offer her some protection should the two men peer round the piece of marble.

"I was under the impression she was waiting until next season." the other man replied. Like his friend, she did not recognise the voice.

"She says that, but the girl will soon change her mind."

"What makes you think that?"

Yes, what does make you think that?

"Look over there, my friend, and tell me what you see."

Annoyingly, Caroline could not see what direction the man was indicating to, and so her eyes scoured the room looking out for something odd, but she could see nothing at all that seemed out of sorts.

"I see a pair of newlyweds, what of it?"

Ah, so they were speaking of her sister and Sir Ernest.

"Not just a pair of newlyweds," Caroline could just feel the sliminess in the man's tone, "but a pair of newlyweds that Miss Morton has to live with until she is wed."

Her eyes moved now to find her Mama and Liam, who were in the same spot she had left them.

"Did you see them earlier?" the man continued. "Miss Morton was with them, and the duke had the gall to kiss his wife. In public! The girl could not run away fast enough."

"What has that to do with anything."

"If they behave like that in public, just imagine what they are like in private."

A pit began to form in her stomach at his words.

"Not only that, but she has nowhere to escape to. Her sister will be the same, and as far as I am aware, the only close familial relations that are unwed are her brother and Duncan Wexford."

"Ah," Caroline winced at the recognition in the other man's voice, "a child and a rake, neither of which will want much to do with her."

"Precisely, she will find herself so lonely by the end of the season that she will desperately accept the first man who approaches her. That, good man, is when I shall be ready to pounce."

"Not if I get there before you."

Caroline cringed at their laughter and startled to sidle away from them.

They were wrong, she thought, in thinking that she could possibly be so lonely. For one thing, she had found no trouble being with Anne and Liam over the past month. Why should she now?

Of course, she had her sister with her then, a little voice in the back of her mind said. Not only that, but her mother and stepfather had been more affectionate in the past few days, and that showed no signs of stopping.

No! Caroline gave her head a shake. She refused to allow those two ghastly men to get into her head. From her position now, she could see who they were.

She was even more astounded at their nerve now, for she had never met either man in her life! How dare they discuss her like a prize cow for them to claim when they deem suitable.

They would have quite the surprise when she spurned them later on.

Seeing her cousin Connie not far away, Caroline made to join her. She would surely find the nerve of the men amusing.

She paused in her step, however, upon realising who Connie was engaged in conversation with. Caroline spotted her cousin's husband, Matt and his wife, and Harry and *her*.

She suddenly felt rather odd about joining such a group, being the only unmarried one.

Looking about the room again, Caroline saw nothing but happy couples. She did not know quite where to go.

Her eyes landed once more on the two men, who had now been joined by another pair, and the four were laughing riotously.

She was allowing the dolts to get inside her mind after all. That would simply not do!

Defiantly, Caroline strode across the hall until she reached her sister. If she could handle a prolonged conversation with a pair of sickeningly in love newlyweds, she would find no trouble living with Anne and Liam.

If anything, she was too stubborn to.

Chapter Nine

Two and a half weeks later

Caroline desperately needed to get out of the house!

Sat at the breakfast table, she watched as her mother and stepfather made vomit-inducing eyes at one another. Since Wilhelmina's wedding, it had not been as bad as expected, but she had had Francis with her then.

He had left the day before with Liam's sister and her husband on a fishing trip. Caroline had been invited to join them but declined thinking it was silly for a woman to do such a thing. Now, she thought there was nowhere she would rather be.

She was not even able to visit her sister yet, as she and Sir Ernest had departed a few days earlier on their wedding trip to Brighton. Before that, Anne had explicitly ordered Caroline not to bother the newlyweds and to stay away for an entire month upon their return.

It was almost as though she thought Caroline would not leave her sister alone. That was only half true, for she would have only bothered her during the day.

That would not stop her though, she decided. But working out the logistics of sneaking visits was of little consequence at the current time for Caroline. Right now, she had to get out of the house!

"The weather is looking rather splendid this morning." she airily stated, causing the married pair to turn and look at her.

"Pardon?" Liam said, blinking in confusion.

"I said that it is looking particularly lovely outside today." Caroline rolled her eyes. "I think I might go for a nice long walk to take advantage of it."

"Quite right, dear." Anne nodded. "Some sun will do you good. Just remember to take a hat with you."

"Would that not defeat the purpose of my taking a walk to begin with?" Liam snorted at Caroline's confusion.

"I meant so you do not burn if you are going out for a longer time than you are used to."

"Because lord knows, we would not want to have to put up with a freckled face across the dinner table each day."

"You would love it," Caroline grinned at her stepfather, "another excuse to tease me."

"I deny anything of the sort." he jested in return "I simply prefer to have pretty things decorate my table."

"We are pretty things now?" Anne smirked at her daughter. "I suppose we should not speak either, so that our looks are not ruined by movement."

"What a splendid idea, wife. That way Francis and I can spend our meals discussing more important matters."

"Ah yes," Caroline contributed, "horses and land, the most important topics of conversation."

"Most certainly." Liam solemnly nodded but the moment his eyes met his wife's, he burst into laughter. "You know, if my sisters were here, I would have received at least four slaps by now."

"I do not need to resort to violence," Anne remarked, toying with her food, "I have far more effective means of silencing you."

At that, Liam's face dropped, and Caroline prepared for yet another round of obvious hints to topics she knew they did not think her ready to be privy to.

"I believe I have eaten enough." she announced, refusing to listen to another round of flirtation. "I think I shall go now, to take advantage of the sun."

"Oh," Anne said in surprise, "if you like, we can join you. Perhaps the fresh air will do us all some good."

"NO!" Caroline shouted a little too hastily, causing her mother to shirk back in her chair. She grimaced at her tone and immediately softened her voice. "I like to take in the scenery and think to myself."

She had never done that in her life, and Anne knew it. At least, judging by her disbelieving look she did.

"Are you quite sure?"

"Yes, Mama." Caroline smiled. "I shall take one of the maids as a chaperone, so I will be quite safe."

"That was not my chief concern."

"Good to know you care little about my welfare." Caroline joked as she stood and moved to kiss her mother's cheek. "Enjoy your day, I do not know how long I will be."

With that, Caroline left the room as quickly as she could without gaining comment, pretending not to hear her mother calling after her.

Readying with haste, she was able to leave Ainsworth House less than five minutes later and walked at a brisk pace until she felt there was enough distance to prevent the pair from catching up to her if they decided to follow.

Slowing down, her maid, Alice, let out a sigh of relief.

"If you do not mind me asking, Miss, are we heading anywhere in particular?"

"I do not care where we go, just as long as it takes us a very long time."

"I thought so." the girl said, sounded rather resigned. Caroline felt a tinge of sympathy for her, in the two- and a-bit months since she had moved into the house, no doubt the maid had borne the brunt of her stubbornness.

She made a mental note to provide her with a little of her pin money to compensate her for having the misfortune of working for her.

"Do you think we shall find many people along the Serpentine."

Alice frowned as she thought for a moment. "It is early, Miss. If you are hoping to meet someone, you would have better luck later on."

Caroline pursed her lips as they continued on in silence, hoping there would be no one looking to disturb her.

"Miss?"

She was interrupted from her thoughts not far from the entrance to Hyde Park.

"Yes, Alice?"

"When you asked if there would be many people there, was it because you wanted to run into someone, or you do not want to?"

"How very astute of you." Caroline smiled. "I just desire a little peace and quiet, that is all."

"Do you wish me to walk a little behind you, then? So as to give you some space?"

"No, as long as we both are quiet, I think it shall be alright but thank you for the offer, nonetheless."

With that, the pair fell into a comfortable silence, strolling alongside the river. Unfortunately for Caroline, the further into the park they went, the more people there were.

It appeared that she was not the only one who decided to take advantage of how bright the weather was, for it seemed that every few seconds she was greeting one person or another.

Just as irritating was the fact that the park was positively bursting with happy couples. Well, not entirely happy judging by a few married pairs she saw out with their overenthusiastic children.

Nonetheless, it was becoming abundantly clear that she was one of the few visitors on their own. The very thing she was trying to escape from she had made ever worse!

Just as trying were the looks on a few of the faces upon finding her out with only a maid. As Ada Duchannes introduced Caroline to her fiancé, her face flickered with sympathy.

"You know, Miss Morton," she whispered to Caroline, "Edwin's brother will be joining us next season. I confess I have yet to meet the man, but I can do a little investigating for you to see if he would be deemed a worthy suitor."

Caroline muttered some words of thanks. Judging by his brother, she was sure the younger Mr Horton was likely to be similar to all the gentlemen she had already encountered in society.

At least this one would come with a sister-in-law she thought agreeable, though.

"I can offer no promises," she asserted, "but if you wish to arrange an introduction at that time, I doubt I shall have reason to refuse."

Ada gave a nod of understanding before her voice returned to her usual volume as she enquired after Wilhelmina.

"We expect a letter any day now from Brighton." Caroline answered. "I imagine it shall continue with the blissful words she has been using as of late. Married life seems to agree with her very much."

"That is good to hear, I know I should not gossip but the way I hear my Mama talking sometimes makes me think that half of marriages are miserable from the off."

"Well, I hope you are in the lucky half." Caroline laughed, indicating her head towards Mr Harper, who was busy looking off into the distance.

Ada's eyes widened and her hand went to her mouth to hide her laughter.

"Trust me, we will be." With that, she directed a wink at Caroline, and burst into another round of giggles.

Before Caroline could enquire as to her meaning, Mr Harper decided to make his voice known.

"I say Miss Morton," he said, his face still turned away from the ladies, "is that not your maid just there?"

Looking in the direction he was pointing his cane towards, Caroline gasped in horror upon seeing Alice lying on the grass, with a crowd forming around her.

Rushing to the girl's side, she was relieved to find that Alice was conscious.

"What happened?" Caroline demanded, staring manically into her maid's eyes.

"She tripped over a duck." an onlooker said, giving Caroline pause.

"A duck?" she asked, confusion etched onto her features. "How does one trip over a duck?"

"Without meaning to, Miss." came the maid's sheepish reply.

Trying not to laugh at the girl's embarrassment, Caroline assisted Mr Harper in helping Alice to her feet. The moment she was upright, she let out a sharp cry.

"My foot!" she shrieked, now hopping on one foot.

"Probably twisted her ankle." Mr Harper decreed. "Do you have far to walk?" he asked Caroline.

"I think it is at least a twenty-minute walk, but with Alice's foot......" her voice trailed off, and Caroline felt tremendously guilty for having dragged the maid out with her this morning.

"Righty-o." Mr Horton nodded before sweeping the shrieking girl into his arms and beginning to walk off. After a moment of being frozen in shock, Caroline ran after the man, demanding an explanation.

"My reticule is not far from here; Ada and I shall take her home on it."

"Oh, thank you." Caroline stammered out in relief. "I shall follow right after you now."

Without saying another word, she turned on her heel and fled in the other direction, determined to rush home so that she could help there.

Pausing at the entrance of the park to gather her breath, Caroline stilled in horror: She was without a chaperone!

She told herself to act as naturally as she could manage, for surely frantic young lady running about London on her own would raise some questions.

Now walking at a leisurely pace, Caroline was struck by how freeing it was to not have to worry about having to be accompanied at all times.

In fact, she felt she could do whatever she wished at this moment. Of course, she would return home at once, but it was nice to simply think that she could do anything.

As the walk continued, she thought to herself: *Why should I not do as I wish?* After all, if she were married, she could go about unchaperoned. As could she if she were a man.

Would it not be nice for once in her life to go do something without having to get permission first?

With that thought, Caroline pondered what it was she would like to do. She considered going to buy something, but that was no good, for anything she would want to purchase, she could go and do so quite easily. That and going for a walk were the things she could do without really asking, just arranging for a chaperone and informing Anne that she was going out.

No, whatever she did, it would have to be interesting and quite possibly daring. But also, Caroline considered, it would have to be a task she could easily accomplish without drawing any attention.

Unfortunately, that seemed to exclude any activity that involved the ton, or else she would surely be ruined.

She was half tempted to venture into the less genteel parts of London, but knowing Caroline's luck, that would result in her being kidnapped and held for ransom or forced to do unspeakable things that she never knew existed,

With a huff, Caroline decided that the only adventurous thing she could do was to continue on the same walk home she had done countless times before, only this time on her own.

That decision lasted approximately fifteen seconds, for she saw a street that she was certain she was familiar with.

A smug smile began to form upon her face and Caroline quickly glanced about to ascertain if anyone was watching her.

Striding with purpose, she stopped in front of a townhouse, quite similar to most other ones in Kensington, and knocked on the door.

An aging butler opened it and showed no sense of surprise that an unaccompanied young lady might be calling on his master.

"Can I help you, Madam?" he asked. Caroline did not feel it needed to correct him for assuming she was married.

"Is Lord Duncan at home this morning?"

"Who might I ask is calling?"

"Caroline Morton."

She waited on the front step whilst the man went to inform her irritating cousin that she was there.

He cannot possibly avoid me now!

The door was then thrust open, and Caroline found herself being pulled into the house as a hand tightened around her forearm.

Regaining her footing, she looked up to find Duncan staring wildly down at her.

"What the devil do you think you are playing at?"

Chapter Ten

Duncan was incredulous at the nerve of the girl in his arms. He thought he would be enjoying a pleasantly simple day with no obligations to worry over.

Instead, before he had even finished dressing, he had been forced to run downstairs and pull the foolish girl inside before she garnered any more attention than she most probably already received.

Without giving her the chance to answer his question, Duncan practically dragged Caroline into the morning room and deposited her in an armchair.

Ignoring her look of innocent confusion, he went and poured himself a generous serving of port, the time of day be damned!

Downing half the glass, he turned and began to pace in front of her.

"I could throttle you right now!" he began ranting. "Do you realise what sort of a position you have put the both of us in? What if someone saw you, dawdling on my doorstep unaccompanied? Even if I had not let you in, you could have ruined yourself. I always knew you had something about you, Caroline Morton, but I did not think it was sheer foolishness."

"Duncan......"

"Why me?" he continued, ignoring her attempt to interject. "Is this to be my punishment for my many sins? To be shackled to the most stupid girl in all of London? I swear to God, Caroline, if I have to wed you because of this, I will take great pleasure in putting you over my knee!"

"I am sorry." came the timid reply. Duncan turned slightly to point his finger at her as he continued but instantly regretted it.

Caroline was staring down at her fidgeting hands, silent tears falling down her cheeks. Duncan detested disappointing or upsetting women, and so regretfully stopped his tirade and lowered himself into the chair beside hers.

"What did you expect, Caro?" he asked gently, reaching into his pocket for his handkerchief only to find it had been one of the casualties of his rush to the door.

"I just missed you." She said, wiping her nose with one of her gloved hands.

Duncan's eyes narrowed as he tried to comprehend her words.

"You missed me?" She nodded in confirmation. "I thought you found me irritating."

"I do but in a friendly way," she looked up at him doe-eyed, her tears thankfully having begun to disappear, "and I have been feeling so lonely as of late. I missed having you there to cheer me up, even if it was by annoying me."

Never in a million years did Duncan ever think that Caroline Morton would be so wistful for his company.

"Come along now, life cannot be that bad for you to wish for *my* company. After all, do you not have your loving family around you?"

"It is not that I am alone, I just feel it." Her hands outstretched towards him, pleading him to understand. "Everywhere I look, I find myself constantly surrounded by people who are married…or engaged…. or courting…...and I just feel as though I am missing something."

"I doubt anyone is purposely trying to make you feel so." Duncan offered. "Besides, would you not rather wait to find someone who makes you truly happy?"

"Oh, I know. It just does not help that, for the single season I have had, you have always been there. I suppose it simply had an effect having you suddenly avoiding me."

"That is not true!" *Yes, it is.*

"Really Duncan?" Caroline gave him a disbelieving look. "Do you seriously expect me to believe that your sudden disappearance had nothing to do with me?"

"I have been busy writing my book." That was half true, at least. "You know the world does not revolve around you, Caro. Or at least I do not."

In truth, he had been avoiding her. It seemed that every time Duncan thought he had his desires for the girl under control, he would see her, and they would become overpowering once more.

He thought the best solution would be to withdraw entirely, focusing solely on his book and the women he preferred. Not that it was working very well.

"I am still not sure I believe you. I do believe this is the first time we have spoken since my sister's engagement ball."

"I remember it more as the event where you were distressed and would not tell me why."

Duncan was pleased at the blush that rose on her cheeks in response and tilted his head to try and prompt her to finally give an explanation.

He waited patiently in silence as Caroline appeared to have an internal debate over whether or not to tell him. Just as it seemed he would not have an answer, she began.

"In truth, I do not know quite what happened."

"What is that supposed to mean?"

"No one ever explains anything to me," she complained, "saying I am too young, or I shall know when I am wed. But it just means I see and hear things that I do not understand and am in a constant state of bewilderment."

Oh god!

Duncan swallowed; fairly sure he knew roughly at least which direction this was heading.

"Perhaps if you describe it to me, I can advise a little bit."

Why did he ask that? He knew he was about to hear something that would only fuel his obsession further.

"Well," she hesitantly started, "I was in the gardens and heard a noise. I thought it was a lady in peril, so I went to investigate."

Oh god!

"Then, I saw Mama with her back against the wall. She was moving in the most peculiar manner."

There it was. Duncan could see clearly in the girl's face the same arousal he had seen in his cousin's office that night.

"I looked down and saw a pair of gentleman's legs sticking out from under her skirts."

"I do not suppose they were kneeling away from her, were they?"

Caroline shook her head.

"It was just so strange. Liam had his head underneath her skirts and Mama was moaning."

That did it. Duncan grabbed the nearest cushion and tried to hide his arousal without being noticed.

He wished he had never pushed her to explain. He was half close to ravishing this poor, innocent girl who had no clue what was going on.

Of course, said girl was innocent but astute and her eyes narrowed at Duncan.

"You know what they were doing."

"Whatever could you possibly mean?"

"Oh please, Duncan," she laughed, "you are supposed to be the most notorious rake in London. Do not play the innocent fool now."

"Never!" he protested. "That is your job." He was satisfied to see the whisper of a smile on her face, though she tried to deny it.

"Innocent, yes. Fool, definitely not."

"You are the one who has entered the home of a notorious rake completely unchaperoned."

He leaned back in his seat, a hand coming to leisurely rest behind his head as he looked smugly at her.

"You could have left me on the doorstep. Denied me entry. But you did not." Caroline returned his smug look with one of her own.

"Miss Morton, you are playing with fire, and you know it."

"Then toss me out onto the street to save yourself."

"Firstly, we do not know that you were seen. Ergo, we may not have to worry at all."

"And secondly?"

"If the most dreaded scenario of our scandalous meeting were public knowledge and I did not marry you, my entire family would take great pains to end my life. I value my hide; therefore, I shall wed you."

"Why continue to prolong the risk then?"

Because I want you in my bed.

"I have a weakness for upset maidens." he lied.

"No, you do not!" Caroline balked. "Unless said maiden is a close relative, you could not stay far enough away. You pride yourself on it."

"I also pride myself on DISCREET STAFF," he raised his voice to ensure they knew of his displeasure at them leaving the girl waiting on his doorstep for all of London to see, "but it cannot work all the time."

"And so, you are resigned to whatever fate awaits you now?"

"One cannot have things go to plan all the time now, can one?"

"What was your plan for the day before I ruined it, then?"

Duncan had no intention of telling her about his original plans for the day, they were far too salacious. A wicked look must have crossed his face, however, as Caroline turned beet red, and her head shot down to stare at her hands once more.

"Duncan?"

"Yes?"

"Would you…...."

A commotion just outside the door prevented whatever her question was from leaving her lips, and Duncan had barely a second to stand before it burst wide open.

Behind it, panting heavily with the wildest eyes he had ever seen, was Caroline's stepfather.

Duncan was not surprised. He was somewhat pleased though.

"Bristol!" he heartily greeted the man. "Come take a seat. Is my lovestruck cousin with you?"

The man's hand raised, and his finger began to frantically dart between Duncan and Caroline, who was shrinking as far into her seat as she could. After a moment, it came to rest on Duncan.

"YOU will marry her!" The Duke was positively foaming at the mouth.

Duncan started to utter his assurances that the girl's honour would not be ruined when her courage suddenly returned to her, and she hurled herself between the pair.

"Liam, please," she pleaded, "it was all my fault. Do not subject Duncan to a lifetime of misery because I have been a fool."

"Really, Caroline, you are not that bad!" Duncan quipped.

"You see," she continued, ignoring him, "Alice tripped over a duck and could not walk, Mr Horton volunteered to take her home and I rushed off to meet them there, not thinking about how I was now unchaperoned until it was too late. I passed by on my way and thought to annoy Duncan. He has been so angry with me and told me off for my foolishness. You cannot possibly punish him for my mistake."

She finally stopped to take a breath and Duncan was quite confused. Her stepfather was pinching the bridge of his nose, whether it was in irritation or defeat, Duncan did not know.

"I am sorry, I cannot get past the bit about the duck."
And who the devil is Mr Horton?

"Caroline," the Duke sighed, "you were seen by Baroness Clarke."

"That will do it." Duncan turned to the confused girl. "Sorry, little one, we have no choice. Best take a good look around, this will be your home soon."

A thought came to him then, a wicked thought. No doubt it would distress Caroline, but he had been distressed in a different way for a much longer time, and so did not feel guilty about suggesting it.

"In fact, given my reputation and the fact that half the ton will be aware of this by now, it is probably best to have the wedding sooner, rather than later." He turned to the bemused looking Duke. "I think with a special license it shall take two weeks at the most."

If you did not know that his two guests were only related through two marriages, their jaws dropping in synchronisation with one another could have made you think otherwise.

Chapter Eleven

Caroline had sat stupefied for the rest of the visit as the two men discussed the details of her impending nuptials.

Her impending nuptials!

Within two weeks, she would be a married woman. She would be Lady Duncan Wexford. She had made the impossible happen and had to stare out of the window for the moment, certain she would see a pig flying past.

After two cups of tea, one of which her fiancé had added a drop of whiskey to whilst her stepfather was distracted, they were ready to leave.

Duncan had taken her hand and planted a kiss upon it. Caroline had thought it rather strange; the temperature was rather warm, yet she had shivered in response.

Sitting opposite Liam in the carriage back to Ainsworth House, she waited for him to say something, but he remained silent for the entire five-minute ride. One peek at the man told her that his jaw was clenched shut, and she became certain that she was to receive the scolding of her life when they returned home.

This was not helped, of course, by the fact that they were immediately confronted by her mother, who was anxiously pacing in the entrance hall.

"What has happened?" she frantically asked them. "What will my cousin do?"

Liam put his arm around her mother and walked them into the drawing room, planting a soothing kiss on her hair as Caroline guiltily traipsed behind.

Her stepfather gestured for both women to sit down. For what felt like the fiftieth time that day, Caroline stared down at her hands, wringing them together. Though she could not see it, she could feel her mother's gaze upon her and did not dare meet the woman's eyes.

"He has agreed to marry her." Liam finally announced, to Anne's audible relief.

"Oh, thank God! We need to announce it soon before the gossip truly takes hold."

"I am arranging the announcement to be in the morning paper, I shall go straight to Fleet Street after lunch to ensure it happens."

"I would have thought an investor in several newspapers would be able to arrange it for the evening paper." Caroline winced at the harshness in her mother's tone, especially as she knew it was all her fault.

"Wexford asked for the time to tell his family in person. He is having dinner with them this evening, so shall inform them then."

Silence fell in the room then. Caroline had no doubt that her mother and stepfather's eyes were now resting on her person. Nonetheless, she kept her gaze unwavering on her gloved hands. Hands that she saw were now quivering slightly.

They stilled when her mother's dainty ones came to rest upon them. Hesitantly, she lifted her head until her eyes met her mothers, and Caroline cringed in preparation for the onslaught.

"Are you well, sweetness?"

That was unexpected, Caroline thought. Instead of a scolding, her mother was worried for her.

"Am I well?" she clarified, still confused when her mother nodded in confirmation. "I have brought scandal to the family, risking my own reputation, and you are enquiring after my welfare?"

"Caroline," Anne exchanged a brief look with her husband before her eyes returned to her stepdaughter's, "you have been my daughter since the age of nine, I should think I would know if you had done something such as this intentionally."

"But I did. I realised I was unchaperoned, and my mind immediately went to deciding what I could do. Then, I saw Duncan's home and made up my mind. This is all my fault!"

"I blame the duck." Caroline looked to her stepfather, who had a sympathetic smile on his face, and she was grateful at his attempt to cheer her up.

"Mama," she said, turning back to Anne, "this is all entirely of my own doing, I have to atone for it."

"We can always find a way to change things." Her mother offered. "If you do not wish this marriage to go ahead, we will use all the resources at our disposal to help."

"I think if we tried that, it would just end up with Duncan kidnapping me and forcing us to wed." The corner of her mouth turned upwards at the thought. "A rake your cousin may be, but he is an honourable one, if that is even possible."

"Caroline," Liam said, crouching before her, "you do know he will not be an easy man to be married to?"

Her lips pursed as she considered what he was saying. "I know he likes to tease and annoy me a great deal, but I am more than capable of returning the favour."

"No, we all know you can hold your own against him. I mean, sweetheart, that Wexford will not necessarily be a loyal man to be wed to."

That only confused Caroline further.

"What Liam means, my love," Anne interrupted, "is that my cousin is known for his reputation with the women of the ton. Oftentimes, men like that do not change their ways just because their ring is on a woman's finger."

"Therefore, I should not expect any loyalty from my husband?"

"Not just that," Liam answered, "but you must be prepared for the differences with the other marriages that surround you. Most marriages in society are business arrangements, but it has become apparent that our family and the Wexford's are different."

"I do not understand."

"Caro, the closest people in your life are going to have a happiness and contentedness in their marriages that your own will be missing."

"Because he will go to other women?"

"Yes," Anne said, "but there is also love."

Caroline considered her mother's words for a moment. This was the thing that had made her feel so terribly lonely, being surrounded by couples deeply in love with one another.

Even so, she thought, was it not the case that before she would have felt a little less lonely if Duncan had not been avoiding her? Indeed, he most likely would have joined her in some light-hearted jesting about how blissful everyone around her was.

That gave Caroline some much needed reassurance, and her face broke into a smile, much to the confusion of her mother and stepfather, who both blinked in surprise.

"That may be the case," she began, "but Duncan has always been my friend. As long as he remains so, I think I shall be quite well."

The couple before her shared a glance, then turned back and offered words of agreement and comfort.

All would be well; Caroline would make sure of it.

Duncan spent the rest of the morning and a good deal of the afternoon sat in his office, failing to put pen to paper. His thoughts were too busy being plagued with Caroline Morton.

It was only natural that they be a mixture of irritation and arousal at the girl. Irritated that she had forced them both into this situation in the first place, arousal at how he would soon have her in his bed whenever he wanted her, and irritated that he was aroused by her to begin with.

After God knows how many hours of failed writing, he threw his quill down and decided to make himself ready for supper with his family.

It was a little early, yes, but Duncan thought it best that he should seek some advice before the dreaded confrontation with the Wexford clan.

And so, a mere seven and a half hours after becoming engaged, Duncan arrived at the London home of the Chalmer's family and waited in their parlour a good three quarters of an hour before his sister made an appearance.

"Kept me waiting long enough." He grumbled the second she walked into the room, not giving her the chance to offer her greetings.

Connie looked as irritated as he felt.

"Excuse me for not being ready to entertain when I have two children to put to bed as I get ready to dine with our family in an hour."

"I thought you had a nanny."

"One would think that after being raised by our parents, you would be more used to the concept of being involved with raising your own child."

"Yes, but Mama always had us put to bed by Nanny when she had engagements."

"No, she had you and Harry put to bed those times because you were a nuisance."

Duncan thought a moment before responding.

"Fair enough."

"Now," Connie said, "are you going to tell me the reason for this surprise visit? Or do you wish to continue being an irritant?"

"I will never stop being an irritant to you, sister dear." Duncan grinned. "Besides, I decided to come here as I thought we might share a carriage to our parents' home."

Connie bit her lip and narrowed her eyes as she observed him.

"Very well, we just need to wait until Xander is ready. I do not expect he shall be long."

Duncan nodded and then accepted his sister's offer of a drink as they waited. When her back was turned to him to prepare it, he dropped the news.

"By the way, I am going to be married in two weeks."

A slight smile fell upon his lips as the sound of glasses clattering filled the room and his sister whirled round to face him, her eyes wide with disbelief.

"Duncan Wexford, if you dare make that joke to Mama tonight, I shall not be responsible for any actions I might take."

"What makes you think I am joking?"

A pointed look was all he got in return and Duncan had to concede that there was a very good reason for the disbelief.

"I know I had previously sworn of the idea of engaging in carnal relations that were not of the sinful nature, but circumstances have forced me to reconsider."

"Oh no!" Connie exclaimed, falling onto the chaise dramatically. *Was he speaking to his sister or Eliza?* "What did you do?"

"I do not think I actually did anything." He supposed that was true. "A young maiden happened to ruin herself and I was in the near vicinity."

"How near?"

"She was on my doorstep."

"And it was not your fault?"

"I did not ask her to be there!"

"She must have had reason to in the first place."

"Look, Connie," Duncan was exasperated, "I was minding my own business, getting ready for the day, when I was told Caroline was on my doorstep, unchaperoned. I had to get her inside before there were multiple witnesses."

Connie's mouth dropped. She stared, shocked, at her brother without blinking.

Naturally, at that moment, her husband decided to waltz through the door. He looked at the scene before him, then waved his hand in front of his unresponsive wife's face.

"What did you do?" he asked Duncan.

"I announced that I am getting married."

For a moment, Xander was also unresponsive, though his face scrunched up in confusion. Eventually, he nodded.

"That should do it." Then, turning back to his wife, the Earl lightly pushed her backwards on the chaise. Duncan thought the way she quickly sprung back to sit upright was rather impressive.

"YOU ARE MARRYING CAROLINE?"

Duncan winced at her scream, but her husband laughed.

"Caroline Morton?" he asked. Duncan nodded in confirmation. "You know, I ran into Liam not two hours ago. He told me that if he sent word, I was to poison your dinner tonight. It makes sense now."

"Yes, he did rather go into fatherly mode when he burst into my home earlier. I did not think him capable of being so furious."

"As someone who knew him at university, you have no idea."

"Are we just going to ignore the fact that my brother has just revealed he is going to be wed to Caroline?" Connie interrupted the calm exchange. "Our cousin's stepdaughter, Caroline, who has harboured an adoration for our brother for years. That Caroline?"

"Yes, I think that summarises it quite nicely." Duncan answered.

Connie sent her husband a look, then turned back to her brother.

"Can I be the one to tell Mama?"

Chapter Twelve

"I must say, I am positively giddy at the prospect of returning to society. I have been far too bored sitting at home twiddling my thumbs."

Duncan rolled his eyes. "I think that if there is one thing that we can be certain of little brother, it is that you can always find some way to amuse yourself."

Duncan was, as usual, sat in the middle of the Wexford dining table. When he had taken his seat, forty-five minutes earlier, it struck him that this would most likely be the last time the entire immediate family would be gathered before he wed.

At least his mother would no longer be able to bemoan how his solitary unmarried state had caused the table to be occupied by an uneven number.

Harry was sat almost directly opposite him, and his emerald eyes were twinkling with excitement at finally ending his mourning for his rat of a father-in-law.

"Naturally, I can," the younger man responded, "but it has been such a trial having to stay away when such exciting drama has been happening right on our doorstep."

"By drama, I assume you are referring to my older brother?"

Duncan smiled at the woman on his right. Eliza had apparently decided to leave the conversation with the Duchess, Matt and Xander on her side of the table to tease her husband.

Harry, though, was not to be put off in his shameless penchant for gossip.

"Who else?" he said. "If you had told me not five months ago that my reclusive cousin would be scandalised into marriage with your newly titled Duke of a brother, I would have eaten my leg!"

"And got splinters in your teeth, no doubt."

"Shut up!" Harry winked at him, and Duncan struggled to contain his smile. "The point is, we have missed out on so much being cooped up at home."

"Have you not been privy to both sides of the scandal, though, Harry?" Jane interjected, also abandoning her own conversation with the Duke and his sister.

In fact, Duncan noted, it seemed that the entire table had decided to join in on the conversation. Most likely as it pertained to their close relative. He felt the opportunity begin to arise to announce his own piece of gossip.

"Being in the know with both our family and my wife's is only half the fun. I miss seeing the looks on people's faces as they are scandalised by the newest gossip."

"You look positively wistful as you think of it, son." their father contributed, amused at his youngest son.

"Regardless," Matt said, "Duncan has apparently decided that the ton cannot handle having all three Wexford men out at once and has been preparing for you to replace him."

At that, eight heads turned to stare at the man in question, and Duncan had it in mind to give his brother a punch at the next available opportunity.

"You are skipping society functions?" Eliza asked in confusion. "That does not sound like you."

"Perhaps our rakish brother has some gossip of his own to impart." Connie suggested, taking a sip of her wine to hide her impish grin.

Duncan narrowed his eyes at her, trying to think of the appropriate punishment to dish out for that.

"Perhaps I do." he said through clenched teeth.

"Just promise me that, whatever it is, you will consider if it is appropriate for the dinner table." his mother advised.

"I think it very appropriate," he said, gathering every inch of courage in his body, "there is to be an announcement in the morning paper regarding myself."

"What did you do?" the Duke asked, sharing a concerned look with his wife.

"I am engaged to be married."

Duncan slammed his eyes shut the moment the words left his lips. His entire body stiffened in preparation for the onslaught.

All he received was silence.

Peeking one eye open slightly, he saw everyone simply staring at him. Opening the other, Duncan looked and realised that not one single face showed a hint of believing him to be speaking the truth.

Well, that was not entirely correct. Connie and Xander both appeared to be doing their utmost to conceal their amusement at his news. Meanwhile, everyone else simply appeared irritated.

"What?" he asked. "Why is Mama not crying? She always cries at news like this."

"This is not an amusing jest." his father sternly responded.

"Who says that I am jesting?"

"Not two days ago you were loudly proclaiming that hell would freeze over before you would marry." Matt added.

"Yes, well," Duncan awkwardly shrugged, "things change."

"What could have possibly caused such a drastic change in the space of two days? That is never enough time for such a change"

"Did you really just say that to a historian?" Duncan sarcastically replied, growing ever more irritated at his family's refusal to even consider the prospect.

"Duncan." He turned upon hearing the soft voice of Jane. "What has happened?"

Judging by the worried look on her face, finally someone was believing him.

"I may have landed myself in a spot of bother, and it was suggested by an irate guardian that there was only one solution that would leave me with breath in my body."

"That is not possible!" Harry said. "You never go near any women who would have a guardian to defend them. We have all heard it enough times: only widows or married women."

"This was the exception."

"*Duncan!*" his mother cried out. "How could you do such a thing?"

"We raised you better than this, son." his father added.

"I did not do anything to ruin anyone." he protested. "She showed up on my doorstep unaccompanied and was seen by a bloody busybody."

"Why would a young lady just appear on your doorstep without a chaperone?" Confusion was etched onto Matt's features.

"We have a......familiarity of sorts."

"A familiarity?" He nodded at his mother's question. "Duncan, who have you become engaged to?"

He stared down at his plate, cringing as he gave his reply.

"Caroline."

Silence.

Silence.

Silence.

"CAROLINE?"

Everyone seemed to shout at once, their faces dumbstruck at the news.

"Caroline Morton?" Matt asked.

"The very same."

"But Caroline's in love with Harry."

"WHAT?" Eliza loudly asked.

"Caroline harboured an infatuation when we were children." Harry quickly reassured his wife. "I have seen her recently and it is quite obvious that she no longer feels the same."

"None of that matters at this moment!" The Duchess' gaze was unwavering on her middle son. "I swear, if you are playing a cruel joke on us, Duncan, you shall very much regret it."

"This is not a joke, Mama. Caroline Morton is to be my wife."

Duncan watched as his mother's face flittered from disbelief to understanding to.......

"Oh god!" he let out. "It is happening!"

Without a moment's hesitation, he rose from his seat and moved to kneel at his mother's side. Now that she fully realised that her last unmarried child was to wed after years of denying he would ever do so, she was sobbing louder than he had ever heard.

"Mama, please." Duncan pleaded. "This is a happy thing......I think."

She spluttered out some unintelligible noises in response.

"I know, Cora dear, but this would hardly be the first time one of our children has had to marry from scandal." the Duke said from where he knelt at her other side.

"How could you possibly understand what she just said?" Duncan asked, bemused. His father ignored him and continued to reassure his wife.

Duncan looked at his siblings, who all appeared to be just as perplexed as he was.

"I recall, brother," Harry said, grinning, "telling you a month ago that you and your intended were rather well suited."

"You did." Duncan reluctantly admitted as he soothingly rubbed his mother's back.

"You were most hostile to that suggestion, were you not."

"As I said before, *little brother*, things can change."

"Well, I for one agree." Connie added. "I believe the pair of you will be most entertaining on nights like these."

"I am most excited to see my brother play the role of the threatening father-in-law." Eliza smirked. "Tell me, Duncan, was Liam terribly mad at your having compromised his stepdaughter?"

"She compromised herself!" he protested once more. "I just happened to be the closest casualty."

"I have barely had the opportunity to speak to Miss Morton. I anticipate speaking with the woman who tamed Duncan Wexford very much."

"It is not possible to tame my brother." Matt told his wife. "They will simply continue to butt heads as they have done since the first day they met."

Duncan felt his mother's hand come to rest on his forearm.

"She will make you the most wonderful wife." she sniffled. "Caroline is such a sweet girl."

"You only get to witness her best behaviour. I, on the other hand, am always there for her worst." he teased.

"One would think that you were the cause of it." Xander responded, earning himself a light slap from Eliza.

"Your brother is right," the Duchess nodded to Harry, much to Duncan's chagrin, "the pair of you are so well suited for one another."

"Have you spoken to Anne yet?" Matt asked. "I cannot think that she will be happy at all the attention this is going to bring."

"Any objections our cousin has matter very little now. I have promised to marry the girl and my honour dictates that nothing will stop me."

"I just hope she is prepared for the onslaught, is all." Matt's hands lifted in defence. "All of London is going to be abuzz over your marrying and both Anne and Caroline are going to bear the brunt of their questions."

"It appears we chose the perfect time to return to society, Liza dear." Harry winked at his wife. "Everyone will come to us for all the gossip."

"In that case, brother," Duncan turned to the younger man, "you best start planning your notorious pranks now. I shall need all the distraction you can make."

Harry grinned in response, always happy to cause mischief.

With that, the entire table burst into heated discussions over what the potential fallout from his marriage would bring. As Duncan began to rise to return to his seat, he felt his mother's hand keep him in place.

"I am so happy for you, dearest." she whispered. "I think you shall have a happier marriage than you expect."

He considered her words for a moment. A glance at his father told him that the man felt the same way.

"You may just be right, Mama." he finally said. "But do not tell anyone I said that. I shall deny it most profusely."

Giving a kiss to her cheek, he moved back to his seat and resumed his supper, rolling his eyes at his family's thoughts on his marriage.

He had two weeks to busy himself with arranging the sudden nuptials. Once that was over, Duncan would be like the cat who got the cream. God help little Miss Caroline!

Chapter Thirteen

It seemed that there was a permanent knot in Caroline's stomach.

It had only been two days since she had become unexpectedly engaged, and she felt that she was already the subject of all the attention of the ton. The previous day they had no less than eight visitors, all of whom called with the feeblest of reasons and wasted no time in trying to pry any information out of her and Anne.

There was no doubt in Caroline's mind that Liam had not actually needed to go over his books but was simply hiding from the onslaught.

No doubt this afternoon would be even worse, she decided. She was sat in her stepfather's carriage with the man himself, her mother and her betrothed. They were on their way to a garden party being held by some dowager she did not know.

She had tried to convince her Mama to excuse her, but Anne thought it best to attend and get the initial rush of busybodies over with.

Added to this was the fact that it was the first time Anne and Duncan had seen one another since before the turn of events. It seemed to be going well, at least they had been polite to one another.

Duncan did seem to be doing his best to avoid her mother's death glare, though. That brought about another form of uncertainty for Caroline.

Should she do something to show some sort of support for her fiancé? A squeeze of the hand or arm perhaps? Considering the circumstances of their engagement, primarily how it was all her fault, she was not entirely certain if it would be welcome.

Therefore, Caroline sat stiffly in the carriage, trying not to meet anyone's eye as the rest of the company engaged in polite, safe conversation.

Upon their arrival, she was surprised at how her betrothed had quickly moved to assist her out of the carriage. Not only that, but he did not let her hand go, instead placing it in the crook of his arm.

Within five steps of the colourful gardens, she already felt several pairs of eyes on them and found herself squeezing his arm tightly.

"Let the battle commence." Duncan whispered in her ear. Turning to look up at him, Caroline felt instantly soothed by the reassuring glint in his eyes and smiled gratefully.

Taking a deep breath, she nodded to the man, and they made their way into the heart of the battle.

"Lady O'Neill." Duncan said as he greeted their hostess. Anne and Liam had already done so and disappeared.

"Lord Duncan." The elderly woman nodded her head to him before turning her steely gaze on Caroline. She gave an awkward curtsey to the woman, unused to having to do so when on a man's arm.

"Your Ladyship," Caroline somehow managed to say with a clear voice, "thank you for the invitation."

"If I had only known when I sent the invitation that my soiree would be the first sighting of the two of you since your scandalous engagement, I would have made it bigger."

Caroline froze, staring wide-eyed at the grinning Viscountess. She had no clue if the woman was teasing or not.

"Is that your version of offering congratulations, Your Ladyship?" Duncan asked, coming to her rescue.

"That was my contribution to the endless remarks you shall be receiving today." The woman's nose wrinkled in amusement as she went on. "I wanted to be the first to say something."

"The privilege of the hostess, I imagine."

"Naturally."

Caroline still had not spoken. One remark already had her scared out of her wits, and she wanted to run all the way back home.

"Do you know, Miss Morton, what happens when you reach my age?"

Caroline managed a squeak in response. The woman ignored the feebleness of it.

"You have seen everything. This means that, when you reach an age which I am not willing to disclose, you find that a sudden engagement between a young lady and a rake has happened tens of times before and becomes quite unremarkable."

"Unfortunately, I do not think anyone else has caught up with that yet."

"Some new scandal will come and take their attention away soon enough." The woman waved her hand to emphasise her point. "Now, the elopement of your future brother-in-law is simply an anecdote, as is the sudden marriage of your future sister-in-law."

An expression of consideration then crossed the woman's face. "In fact, if you are going by recent events, it will most likely be another Wexford who is at the centre of the next piece of gossip."

"Come along now, My Lady," Duncan's tone was defensive, "we are not *that* bad!"

"Your grandfather dropped dead at my daughter's engagement ball." came the blunt reply. Caroline was forced to cough to hide the giggle she had let out at the unexpected statement.

"And almost thirty years later, people are still talking of the ball, including your daughter."

The Viscountess gave him an unamused look before turning back to Caroline.

"Rest assured, Miss Morton, within the week, people will have something new to talk about. Though, you will still be stuck with an idiotic husband."

With that, she turned away and greeted the next guests in line. Caroline allowed herself to be gently guided away by her fiancé.

"You know," she said to him, "I do believe that I quite like our hostess."

"You would."

This was perhaps the most exhausting party of Duncan's life!

He had remained beside his intended for at least an hour, listening to subtle and unsubtle barbs about their engagement.

At least, he thought, the people making them were entirely unaware that the woman beside him could be just as barbarous as them, and so half of them ended up with wonderfully red faces as they left.

Finally having a moment's peace, Duncan found his thoughts being interrupted by an elbow to the ribs. If it were not for the evil spark in Caroline's eye, he would have said she looked entirely innocent of having done the gesture.

"What were you thinking about?" she asked.

Which statue is best to drag you behind.

"Which flower is likely to make me sneeze the most." he lied.

"Oh. Well, I was just asking where you thought I might find a drink. I feel rather parched and cannot for the life of me see any footmen about."

Caroline was blind, Duncan thought, for he could see one not ten paces away from them. Regardless, he decided to indulge her.

"Wait right here and I shall fetch you a glass."

In return, she offered what he thought to be a breathtaking smile of gratitude and his knees suddenly felt a little wobbly.

Dear god, he thought as he walked away, *I am becoming quite pathetic!*

Looking around, Duncan now realised what Caroline meant. All the footmen were carrying food on their trays, not a single drink.

Luckily, it did not take him long to spot a table filled with refreshments. Standing before it, he reached his arms across to grasp a glass of lemonade when a gloved hand appeared to rest on it.

Thinking that Caroline had decided to heed his order and join him, he turned to face the owner with a beam on his face. The smile faltered from genuine to polite when he saw the woman who was actually standing beside him.

"I was beginning to believe that I would not have the chance to catch you on your own."

Mrs Delilah Thorne was ten years his senior. With her scarlet locks, ice blue eyes and plump lips, he had eagerly taken her to his bed. But that was three years prior, making Duncan wonder what was causing her to seek him out now.

"Mrs Thorne," he greeted her politely, "I had not expected to see you here today."

"I was in half a mind whether to attend, then I heard your surprising news and had to come see for myself that it was true."

"And you find it so. Are you wondering what sort of woman it took to tame me after all?"

Her forehead wrinkled a little in amusement.

"I must confess, I had no idea what to expect. She is quite lovely and undeniably *innocent*."

Duncan awkwardly rubbed the back of his neck; he was beginning to feel a little warm.

"I am not entirely certain if you mean that as a compliment or not." he coughed out. She laughed at his words.

"It was more of an observation. You see," her voice lowered then, "I was speaking to some of my lady friends after hearing the news and there was a decent amount of worry coming from them."

Duncan frowned. "Why should they be worried?"

"That was my thought, I kept telling them that your marrying would not mean that affairs could not continue."

Comprehension began to dawn on him. To be truthful, Duncan had not paid a single thought to what his marrying Caroline would mean for his relations with other ladies of the ton. In fact, he had not thought of other women at all.

"The fact that she does seem so innocent no doubt confirms it." Delilah continued. "You have always made your preferences very clear, and I am pleased to see that you are simply settling down as men often do."

"Am I?"

He could not deny that she was looking at him with obvious lust in her eyes and her hand came back to rest on his arm again.

"I look forward to seeing you again, once you have properly settled into wedded life."

With that, she gave his arm a stroke and left without saying another word. Duncan stared at her retreating form in confusion.

Had he just agreed to another affair?

Still utterly perplexed, he grabbed a pair of drinks and wandered back to Caroline, handing one over when he reached her.

"Who was that you were speaking to?" she asked, causing him to panic.

"No one!" he said a little too fast.

"I saw you quite clearly, you were talking with a red-haired woman. Do you know her well? She is quite beautiful."

"Oh, that woman." Duncan tried not to cringe at how high his voice was. "Casual acquaintance, barely speak to her now, actually."

For a moment, Caroline stared at him in confusion. Then, her eyes widened, and her mouth grew into the most wicked smile.

"But you used to speak to her very much indeed, I imagine."

"I have no idea what you are referring to." That only made her smile wider.

"Of course, I shall play the oblivious maiden."

"You do not need to play it, you are one!" he spat back a little too harshly.

In any case, Caroline paid no mind to it. She simply looked about the gardens, absentmindedly sipping on her lemonade.

"I say," she said out of nowhere, "are there many of your conquests here?"

"Caroline…....." he warned.

"I was simply asking; I would not like to say the wrong thing to the wrong person."

"What you do not know, cannot hurt you."

"What if I come across a spurned former lover of yours who sees my innocent words as goading?"

"Then you shall have a husband who will protect you from whatever may happen." His words were spoken through gritted teeth.

"I shall allow you to believe that."

At that he turned to her, prepared to express his irritation firmly. Instead, he saw the humoured smile on Caroline's face and suddenly burst into one of his own against his will.

"Shut up!"

Chapter Fourteen

"I do not believe I have ever seen my Mama so animated." Duncan proclaimed.

Caroline looked ahead at their mothers and had to smile at how enthusiastically the Duchess was gesturing as she regaled some story to Anne.

"I imagine the Her Grace is simply relieved that her wayward son is settling down at last."

"Only in my family," Duncan balked, "would a man marrying at the tender age of five and twenty be considered a relief to all."

"You must admit that you are rather late compared to the rest of your brothers."

"Nonsense! They are early."

"If you say so."

"I do."

The pair continued to walk on in silence, following the path their mothers were taking alongside the Serpentine.

Soon enough, Caroline recognised the part of the park they had wandered into.

"Be careful," she teased, "people are known to be surprised by ducks in this area."

"Have we come upon the scene of the crime?" Her companion's face took on a faux-serious expression, his eyes darting around with suspicion. "We must be on guard at all times. Have no fear, Miss Morton, I shall defend you with every breath in my body."

"You die to protect me from twisting an ankle, I somehow do not believe those choices are evenly matched."

"Let me have my fun." She felt his elbow gently nudge into her side at that, and could not resist reciprocating the gesture, albeit with a little more force than he used.

Caroline let out a sigh as they fell into a comfortable silence, offering greetings to friends and acquaintances as they passed. Ten full minutes had passed before one of them spoke again.

"I must be going mad." Duncan exclaimed, making her start.

"Do I want to know?"

"Even if you did not, I shall tell you nonetheless." Caroline supressed a grin at his answer.

"Come along, then. What is the cause of the onset of your inevitable insanity?"

"You."

"Me?" She paused in her step, looking at her fiancé in confusion. "Whatever could I have done?"

"Nothing at all. Which is precisely the problem."

"That makes no sense at all."

"Very little in life does." His teasing was beginning to frustrate her.

"If you have no intention of speaking clearly to me, then please let us continue on in silence."

"That is the bizarre thing." Duncan said as they began to move forward again. "Aside from your comment about ducks, you have been for too quiet today. That causes me to worry."

Caroline let out a laugh, much to the man's chagrin it seemed.

"I am being quite serious! You have not made a single comment to tease me today. That is very unlike you."

"I only tease you because you tease me!" she said defensively.

"And I have been teasing you a great deal and have had nothing in return." With his free hand, he covered her own one where it was tucked into his arm. "Please, I implore you, what can I do to get my irritating Caroline back?"

"Stop being silly! I doubt that when we are married, we shall be constantly in conversation with one another. On occasion, some peace is rather lovely."

"Humph."

Caroline rolled her eyes at the man. They continued on for another moment, silent once more, as she debated whether or not to ask him about the topic that had consumed her mind since her discussion with her Mama the previous night.

In the end, her curiosity won out, and she began her timid approach to the topic.

"If you must know, my mind has become a little occupied suddenly."

His brow furrowed. "Whatever for?"

"It is rather delicate. To do with matters of womanhood."

For a moment, Duncan simply looked at her in confusion. Then, comprehension dawned on his features. His eyes widened and briefly flickered downwards towards her most private area, causing Caroline to blush in embarrassment.

"Is it gruesome?" he whispered, leaning his head closer to her own. "You know, many women tend to become irritable during this time. You seem to be the opposite.

Perhaps it is because you are naturally irritable by temperament and your *thing* has calmed you?"

"What?" Caroline frowned in confusion before her own comprehension dawned. "*Duncan Wexford!* If we were not in public, I would slap you right now."

"Come along, Caro. Most men do not even consider talking of it. That must make me already superior."

"Not when you do not even know what I am speaking of."

Duncan's eyes darted about as he tried to understand what she was saying. Seeing that she was getting nowhere letting him work it out for himself, Caroline lowered her voice.

"What I am speaking of is the talk I had with Mama last night about what to expect once I am married."

If there was one topic her fiancé would waste no time in grasping, it was that of the bedroom. And Duncan certainly did not disappoint.

His mouth spread into the most wicked grin and those emerald eyes lazily stalked down her body knowingly. Caroline began to redden once more and felt that strange jolt of anticipation form in her stomach again.

"Your endless questions have been answered at last then?" he teased.

"Not at all. I have more questions than before."

Duncan let out a short boom of a laugh. Knowing he was rather famous for the topic at hand, Caroline felt even more shy.

"There is no need to laugh at me." Her voice was barely more than a whisper. Still, he managed to hear her.

"I am not laughing at you, darling, just how typical it is that you are more confused than ever. It would be the same for most maidens I imagine."

She felt a little soothed, though his endearment ensured that her blush remained in place.

"Now, Miss Morton." Duncan continued. "Providing these questions are not too inappropriate for a stroll, can I answer any of them for you? I do not know if you are aware of this, but I am considered something of an expert on the subject."

"To be honest, that was one of the things I was wondering about."

Out of the corner of her eye, Caroline could see his head tilted at her with interest. She could not bear to look directly at him though, she was too horrified. Instead, she kept her gaze staring straight ahead at she went on.

"Mama said that many women find the act uncomfortable if they do not have a generous partner. Then, she offhandedly declared that I would not have any troubles having you as my husband."

"I must thank Anne when I next have the chance."

"Do not dare!" Caroline shrieked, appalled at the prospect. Of course, he chuckled.

"Have no fear, I shall save you from further embarrassment. But would this not soothe you, my knowing how to make the marriage bed enjoyable for you?"

"How do you know what to do?" she burst out. She was still unconvinced that it was possible for the act her mother described to be pleasurable.

Duncan remained quiet for a moment, causing Caroline to finally swallow her pride and look at him. She thought he looked rather thoughtful at whatever he was considering.

"I suppose it is a multitude of things." he finally said, pausing briefly so they could pass a large family without risking them overhearing the scandalous conversation.

He peered back to ensure they were out of earshot before speaking again.

"I had just turned fifteen when I first bedded a woman, though I suppose you could say she was the one to bed me." He smiled, and Caroline felt a little annoyed as she imagined he was reminiscing over it.

"After we were done, I shyly asked her how she thought I did. She said that it was very good considering. I just needed a little practice. So, I suppose you could say it is partly natural instinct."

"I cannot believe you would ever do something shyly."

"You did not know me as a boy of fifteen."

"Yes, I did!"

"In any case," he continued, ignoring her correction, "I took good old Mabel's advice and practiced. With each and every woman I tupped, I learnt to pick up little things about them."

"What sort of things?"

"Well…." His lips pouted and his eyes narrowed as he considered her question. Caroline was struck by how sweet he looked as he was thinking.

Sweet? That was not a word she would ever think to associate with Duncan Wexford!

"I suppose I simply pay attention." He finally answered. "There are obvious signs that a woman is or is not enjoying herself, as well as subtle signs. One just has to learn to read them."

Caroline was perplexed by the simplicity of it.

"That does not sound particularly difficult," she mused, "I do not know why you should be so renowned for it."

"Miss Morton, how dare you question my knowledge of the fairer sex." he admonished with a smile.

"I question everything you assert about yourself." Caroline teased.

"Now, that is more like the Caroline I know." he grinned. "And if you must know, the reason why less men are renowned for it is because many men do not care to pay attention, they simply think of their own pleasure."

"Men are selfish? How surprising." she sarcastically replied.

"Some are, some are not. The unselfish ones are usually loyal to their wives or discreet. A great deal of circumstances must apply to acquire a reputation like my own."

"If you say so."

"I do. I have worked hard to acquire such a reputation."

"I imagine it was such a hardship for you."

"There was only one hard thing about it." His voice turned to a mutter, but Caroline still picked it up and it sent her into a panic.

"Yes, Mama mentioned that." Her breath began to quicken. "I shall be stripped bare, my legs thrust apart, and you shall stick it inside of me."

"If you want to put it technically."

Duncan was staring at her with concern.

"Caroline, are you well?"

"No, I am not!" she burst out. "Never in my life have I been kissed. I have never been held by a man in any way other than fatherly love and now I am expected to do it all in the space of a few short hours."

"Caroline......" he tried to interrupt her panicked ranting.

"Do you know what makes it worse?" She jabbed her finger in his chest, uncaring if it was witnessed. "You nor any other man will ever understand how it feels. You are allowed to go about as you please seducing women and are praised for it."

He at least had the good sense to look ashamed of it.

"Meanwhile," she continued, "I spend one moment on a doorstep, unchaperoned, and I have no choice but to marry or ruin my family."

"Of course, it is unfair!" Duncan agreed.

"I know what you are going to say about it, that there is nothing either of us can do. That may be true, but it does not help that I am prepared to feel more overwhelmed, and anxious, and terrified than I have ever felt in my entire life."

Duncan stopped, forcing her to pause in her steps also. He was looking at her with an intense seriousness she had not thought possible for him before.

"Caroline Morton." he said, his eyes beseeching her own. "I agree, you are going to feel all those things. Just as all other young ladies in society are forced to do. But you have one thing they do not have. Do you know what that is?"

She shook her head, trying to keep the threatening tears at bay.

"Me."

"How splendid!" she barked at him. "I am so special because I have the greatest lover in London in my bed."

Duncan looked at his feet, smiling in amusement at her, which only served to anger Caroline further.

"No. You have a friend. One who has cared about you since the first moment he laid eyes on the little girl peeking over her shoulder from a church pew."

Caroline was stunned. She could not believe that he would ever have remembered that first glimpse they shared. Nor that he had cared for her for all this time, she always thought that he found her an annoyance, even if they were friends now.

"I understand that our engagement did not come about the usual way, and we most certainly would never have chosen one another. But rest assured, Miss Morton, the thought of hurting you pains me."

She now felt rather out of breath.

"If you wish to take our intimate relations slowly, I would never wish to force you." He expression became both reluctant and disgusted as he went on. "Even if that means that our marriage is not consummated for a great while."

Caroline had no clue how to respond. She was so touched by his words and realised that, truthfully, there was never a point in which she did not feel safe when Duncan Wexford was with her.

Unable to articulate a response, she simply made a tight but grateful smile and nodded her head. He nodded his in return, faced forwards and began to walk once more.

She felt rather more comfortable now than she had been only a few minutes before.

Chapter Fifteen

It just had to be perfect. Duncan's tongue was peeking out of the corner of his mouth as he concentrated on lining the angle of his cue perfectly.

There. The perfect shot. Every inch of him remained perfectly still where he leant over the billiard table. His arm began to slide backwards, dragging the cue with it.

He took a breath and began to thrust forward.

"Dear god, Wexford! Take the shot already."

Duncan buried his head in his arm, tempted to weep at how he had missed the ball completely. Making a strangled noise, he straightened his back and sent a filthy look to his brother-in-law, who laughed.

"You should not have taken so long."

"Keep ruining my game and I shall take no time at all to make my sister a widow."

"Come now," Liam Ainsworth butted in, "if you do that, the rest of us will have to become accomplices to murder."

"Why do we have to do anything? Leave them to it, I say." the Duke's younger brother, Lord Frederick, asked.

"Because this buffoon needs to marry Caroline. He can hardly do that from the gallows."

Duncan chuckled, picking up a stray bottle of wine and drinking straight from it. If his future not quite a father-in-law had something to say about it, then he should not have volunteered to host a bachelor party in his house.

"I second that." Harry called out. "We need to witness the glory that is a Duncan-Caroline marriage, to prevent it would be akin to a grievous insult."

"I think you are more excited for my marriage than I am, brother."

"I am simply returning the favour. I shall not repeat what you asked me about Liza when we first married."

Duncan cringed under Ainsworth's accusatory gaze. He very much doubted the man would be happy to learn he had once asked if the man's sister was 'wetter than an otter's pocket.'

"Are the ladies at home tonight?" he quickly asked, anxious to change the subject. "I can only imagine what Anne would say if she stumbled across all of us, well, stumbling about."

The Duke smiled into his glass at that. "You would be surprised at what does and does not scandalise Annie."

"I do not want to know." Harry dryly said, making the man laugh. He then watched as his friend took his place at the table in front of him.

Duncan was intrigued by the look on the Duke's face and burst into his own laughter as the man lifted his leg and kicked Xander's behind, causing the man to miss his shot completely.

He and Harry exchanged a surprised look when the Earl simply grumbled at his friend before slinking off to have another drink.

"I say!" Harry said, his eyes widening. "Are either of you two going to at least pretend to play fair?"

"No." they both bluntly replied.

Duncan was put off by approximately three seconds until he realised that this meant he could play dirty as well. He quickly began to plan his first act of sabotage.

Seeing his little brother warily look about as he prepared to take his own shot, an idea came to Duncan's head. Who cared if they were on the same team? This was far more fun!

Just as he moved forward, however, a hand appeared on his shoulder, holding him firmly in place. Looking to his right, Duncan found Ainsworth standing so close that he was almost pressed up against him.

"You know, Wexford," he said, his voice low, "a thought came across my mind that, as Caroline's stepfather, I am entirely responsible for her safety and happiness."

The hand on his shoulder began to squeeze.

Hard.

"As I wish to fulfil this duty as best I can, it makes me think that I must inform you of the consequences should any trouble befall on said safety and happiness."

Common sense dictated to Duncan that he had nothing to fear from the Duke, but that did not prevent his heart from speeding up a few beats.

"Not only that, but I happen to like the girl, not just because she is my stepdaughter, but because I find her rather agreeable. Therefore, it should grieve me very much if I bore witness to any upset for her."

Duncan's mind started to race. Ainsworth was a great deal fitter than he was, with an athletic build much more adept to physical exertion than his own portly one. It may be the case that he would need to use his mind to defend himself.

"You know, growing up I had always thought our family estates too close to one another in proximity. Now I find it rather intriguing."

Risking a glance over his shoulder, Duncan was unreasonably petrified by the glint in Ainsworth's eye.

"Now, I imagine it would not cause any displeasure at all if I were to come across you on, say a morning ride."

"I rarely ride." Duncan squeaked.

"I am sure our paths will cross regardless."

With a hard pat on the back, the Duke returned to the game, leaving Duncan stood rooted to the spot, his head darting around the room, certain he would find traps hidden in wait for him.

So caught up in his terrors was he, that he failed to realise that there were new arrivals until the bottle was suddenly taken from his grasp, causing a loud, feminine shriek to emit from his mouth.

Quickly regaining his wits, he saw that the thief was his own father, who was now staring at him in resignation. Behind him, was his uncle, who appeared to be containing his laughter.

"Good evening." Duncan said in greeting, making his voice lower to compensate for his outburst, not that it would do him any good.

"Son." his father nodded. "Your mother still refuses to believe that in a mere four days, you will be a married man."

"Whyever not?"

The elder man stared at him in confusion. "Perhaps because for years you refused to entertain even the slightest notion of marrying."

"Well, I know that! But have I ever been one to break my promises? Surely my saying that I was going to marry was enough confirmation?"

"Did you not promise just yesterday to join Jane and I for supper?" his eldest brother said as he approached.

"Did I?"

"I am afraid so."

"Well, I do not remember doing so." Duncan waved the critique aside. "I certainly remember saying I would wed Caroline. Therefore, you should all trust that I shall follow through on that promise."

"I shall keep the names of those who have wagered against it hidden then."

"What?" Duncan called after his father, who had wandered off in the direction of food.

"I cannot believe my little brother is getting married." Matt commented.

"Are people really betting on whether I make it to the altar or not?"

"Not necessarily." Matt answered, after thinking for a moment. "If I recall correctly, there is one where you go into a panic upon hearing 'til death do you part' and run off in a terrified frenzy."

"That does not sound like me."

"Obviously, you do not know yourself as well as the rest of us do."

Duncan narrowed his eyes at his brother, irritated that wagers were being placed on him. He stretched his now-empty hand and decided he was vastly in need of another drink.

"Have you come to terms with it yet?" his brother asked, preventing him from seeking out his wants.

"What?" Duncan responded, thoroughly irritated.

"Your feelings for your intended?"

"And what feelings would those be?" he played the fool. In the past months, he had refused to admit how he lusted after the girl no matter how many times his brother pried.

"You know damn well what feelings." His brother sent him a knowing look. "You have been lusting after her for months. Now that you are going to marry her, you may as well admit to them,"

"I have no clue what you are referring to. I only have those of respect for Caroline."

"Yes, and the Pope is protestant." Matt sarcastically replied. "You want that girl in your bed, and none of your denials can change how obvious it is."

"If it is as obvious as you say, why are you the only one who has said anything to me?"

"They are all blind......or polite. I am neither. If it is any consolation, I have placed a large wager on your marrying without a hitch."

Duncan looked at his grinning brother and found his resolve wavering. Perhaps if he gave the fool some morsels, he would drop the subject.

"I refuse to admit any sort of lustful feelings towards Caroline, of all people, but I cannot say if that shall not change after my wedding night unfolds."

"You never know," Matt said, "perhaps you will find having an untried woman in your bed to be more enjoyable than you imagine."

Oh, it will!

Duncan gave a noncommittal shrug in answer and excused himself, determined to find himself a drink.

His mission lasted fifteen seconds before falling at the wayside. Once again, he felt a hand on his shoulder. This time he was physically dragged backwards.

"Now, nephew," his uncle began, "I think that we should have a little talk."

"About what, Uncle William?"

"My granddaughter."

Wonderful.

"I believe that I can imagine what you are going to say."

He glanced to his side, finding his uncle's face unreadable.

"Then this little talk shall not take much of our time, and you can go back to your revelry."

"With a little less enthusiasm, you hope?"

The older man chortled a little, but his expression quickly returned to its prior state.

"Caroline may have a prickly exterior, but inside she is such a sensitive soul. I would be most displeased to hear if she received any upset in her new marriage."

Duncan strained a smile and resolved to appeal to the man. "Uncle William, I think you of all people would know that hurting Caroline is the last thing I could ever wish to do."

"Your reputation states otherwise."

"Reputation or not, Caroline has always been, and will always be, my friend and, as such, hurting her would be the last thing I could ever do."

"I hope so." The hand finally left his shoulder. "It would be terrible to see my brother grieve for the sudden and tragic death of his middle son."

Duncan's face was frozen in both horror and resignation. He supposed it was only expected that his uncle would be protective of Caroline, even if it were not by blood, she was his granddaughter through and through.

Stretching his neck to try and get some feeling back into it, Duncan resumed his search for a drink. Whatever it was, he needed a strong one.

Looking about the room, all he could see was bottles of wine and champagne. That was not what he needed.

"Ainsworth!" he approached his host. "Do you happen to have any whiskey about?"

The man's brow furrowed for a moment.

"I normally keep it in my office and the drawing room, but do not dare go in the drawing room! Anne is keeping Caroline firmly ensconced in that side of the house."

"The office then." Duncan nodded. "I shall be back before you know it."

He did not linger, immediately darted off both to get the drink and to have a moment to himself.

Wandering about the halls of Ainsworth House, Duncan had to laugh. If someone had told him only two years ago that he would be freely wandering about the halls with the full permission of the host, he would have laughed in their face. It was funny how things came to pass.

Reaching his destination, he made a beeline for the beautiful amber liquid he craved. Pouring a finger, he savoured the smell as he brought it to his lips. Just as he was preparing to open his mouth to take a taste, a voice broke his concentration.

"What are you doing in here?"

Opening his eyes, he found the eight-year-old brother of his intended looking up at him from the doorway.

"I should ask you the same question."

"This is my father's office; he will be angry when he finds out you have been in here."

Duncan was very tempted to laugh at the furious pout on the child's face.

"Well, Baron Morton, perhaps we could keep this our little secret?"

Fat chance of that, judging by the boy's face. Thank God for once that Duncan had actually asked permission before helping himself to his host's private stash.

"Are you going to be a good husband to my sister?" Francis suddenly said to Duncan's horror.

"Dear god, are you going to threaten me as well?"

Chapter Sixteen

It just had to be perfect. But why did Caroline care so much?

In a mere two days, she would be Lady Duncan Wexford, wearing this very dress. Purple had been decided, for it had always been her colour. Made of tulle with beading along her waist and sleeves, she was worrying it was too much.

Why did it matter to Caroline so much, she wondered? It was not as though Duncan was anticipating anything in particular when they met at the altar. He only saw her as a little girl, after all.

She was stood on a stool, in front of a wide mirror in their dressmaker's shop. Madam Angelique was adjusting the hem of her dress, and Caroline tried to stay as still as she could.

"Providing you smile on the day; you will be the most beautiful bride." Anne said from behind her.

Their eyes met in their reflections in the mirror. Caroline forced a smile, causing her mother to shake her head in the manner only a mother can.

"I think ze dress is ready, Mademoiselle Caroline." the dressmaker said, rising to her feet.

Taking her eyes away from her reflection, she turned to the woman.

"Thank you, Madame, it is quite beautiful."

"You will make a magnifique bride." Madam Angelique smiled. She then turned to Anne to confirm the details of the dress' delivery that evening.

An assistant helped Caroline out of the gown, and the girl felt a pressure almost lifted off her as she stepped out of the material.

Nerves were only natural, Caroline assured herself, especially when the wedding in question was happening so suddenly.

Caroline wondered, though, if she would change any of it, would she?

Her entire life, she had believed she would marry for love. The little she could remember of her real mother, she remembered her and her and Papa being so in love with one another.

It was the same with Papa and Anne, Wilhelmina and Ernest, even Anne and Liam! She had believed for so many years that it would be the same with her and Harry, but they were not meant to be.

Her long-awaited debut in society had been a disappointment. Caroline had been presented with the cream of the crop of the ton, yet none of them were anything that she could imagine falling in love with. The thought of spending her life with one of them was not even something she could consider.

But Duncan was a steady presence in her life. He was someone she could depend on. She was going to marry a man she could call her friend. It was not love, but that did not mean it was not important to her.

Caroline was not going into this marriage with naïve expectations of love and bliss. She bore very little doubt that Duncan would not stray. Nonetheless, she knew she would feel safe with him.

"Are you ready to go, sweetheart?"

Anne's voice brought her out of her reverie. Caroline turned to her Mama and nodded.

They had no more appointments after their visit to the dressmakers, Instead, Wilhelmina offered to host tea for the three of them.

Caroline's sister had returned from Brighton just the day before, cutting her trip short to attend the wedding. Yet another thing for the older girl to feel guilty over.

To her credit, Wilhelmina showed no signs of animosity as she welcomed her mother and sister into her home. Caroline thought her sister seemed to have an ease about her that she had not possessed prior to her marriage.

As the blonde escorted her guests to the orangery, she was describing her marriage trip in full detail without stopping for breath. Caroline and her Mama exchanged an amused look at the younger girl's enthusiasm.

Surrounded by the blooming oranges and yellows of the Fawcett orangery, the trio sat around a small table and Wilhelmina immediately grasped hold of the other women's hands.

"Does it not seem a lifetime ago that we had just arrived in London for the season?" she said with a disbelieving smile. "I can scarcely comprehend how much has changed in just a few short months."

"I had hoped that my wonderful daughters would find their perfect matches," Anne added, "but I cannot believe that I would as well. And all three of us in one season!"

"Who would have thought it possible!" the younger girl nodded.

"The fact that two of those matches were achieved through scandal makes it a little more believable." Caroline snarked, accepting a freshly poured teacup from her sister.

"I suppose I can lord it over you forever, now." her sister grinned. "I was able to wed through a respectable route."

"I shall endeavour to gloat that I tamed the most notorious rake in London then." Caroline retorted, not to be outdone by her younger sister.

"Yes, to think that I was missed the excitement by mere days." Wilhelmina's eyebrows lifted with interest. "Or was it perhaps because I was gone that you felt the need to find yourself someone to save you from your loneliness?"

She supposed that was half true, but Caroline was not about to admit that to someone anytime soon.

"Or could it be that I no longer had the responsibility of keeping you company and could do what I wished for once?"

"Or perhaps we all have our tea without resorting to bickering like unmarried ladies?" Their Mama stopped the sister's teasing in advance.

"Fine." Both girls said in unison.

"If we are being technical about it," Caroline teased, "than I am not a married lady yet."

"Yes, well I doubt your personality shall change too much in two days' time." Anne shook her head.

"It changed well enough after I married!"

"You still seem to be my silly little sister." Caroline observed. "You cannot have changed that much."

"Not me silly. You."

"Me?" Caroline asked, bemused.

"Yes." Wilhelmina said seriously. "Before I married, you would not stop blathering on about how there was no one in all of England interesting enough to tempt you into marriage."

Caroline sent her mother a questioning glance. As her sister continued on with her rambling perceptions, she mouthed "Does she know?" at the older woman. How much exactly did her sister know of the circumstances of her engagement?

Anne's face matched her own confused one. They both gave the younger girl similar glances of befuddlement. It took a moment, but Wilhelmina realised her musings were not getting their intended response.

"What?"

The two older women burst into laughter at the confused look on her face.

"Why are you laughing at me? Do I have something on my face?" Wilhelmina started frantically rubbing her face.

"Mina, stop." Caroline covered her sister's hand with her own, stopping her movements. "You do know the circumstances of my engagement, do you not?"

"That you compromised yourself into marriage by visiting Duncan alone?"

"Yes........." Caroline said the word slowly to try and hint to her sister how contradictory her point was.

Wilhelmina continued to look confused for a moment, then her eyes widened, and her hand covered her open mouth in horror.

"*Caroline!*" she admonished. "What did you do with Duncan?"

"Nothing." Caroline answered, unable to comprehend how dense her sister was being. "I am simply confused as to why you would be saying that I had changed my mind about marrying when the only reason I am doing so is because I have been forced into it."

"I do not see how it is confusing."

"Wilhelmina, dear," Anne tried to reason with her now, "you do understand that none of this is of your sister's choice?"

"If Caroline did not desire to marry at all, why would she do something so obvious like lingering on a single gentleman's doorstep in the middle of the day for all to see?"

Truthfully, Caroline did not know if she could make a decent argument against that. She knew well enough the consequences of being caught in such a position, and she still took the risk, albeit spontaneously.

"It was actually early in the morning." she pathetically murmured.

"That is even worse." Wilhelmina smirked. "In any case, if you had refused to marry Duncan, it is not as though anyone could do anything about it."

"Other than mark me a ruined woman."

"With your pretty looks, large dowry and familial connections to two ducal families, I very much doubt many men would drop out of the race for your hand."

Caroline looked at her mother, who was clearly struggling to supress laughter. After all, was this not what Anne and Liam were suggesting when they returned from Duncan's residence that fateful morning?

"Perhaps, in that moment, I realised that I would have more freedom as a married woman and took the opportunity." she fibbed. "Not to mention that I am doing Duncan quite the favour by marrying him."

"Why is that?" Anne asked, intrigued.

"By finally marrying, he will no longer have to worry about pressures from his mother or being trapped into marriage by ambitious young ladies."

"You mean like he has been?" Wilhelmina teased.

"Duncan is not complaining." Caroline retorted. "I think he shall be the most agreeable husband."

"Mama, are you listening to this? Our Caroline has found someone who she approves of for marriage. Has some sorcery been cast?"

"Why should I not find the man agreeable? He is my friend and will allow me to go about my life with no objections."

The younger woman looked at her thoughtfully for a moment.

"And what if you should find a man whom you love? Who you would have willingly married without scandal?"

"One thing I have been told over and over again has been that I should not expect any sort of loyalty from my husband." Caroline gave a sly smile. "By that logic, I should feel free to have my own affairs."

The sound of teacups clattering greeted that announcement, and the look of sheer horror on her mother and sister's faces was simply perfect.

"Caroline Morton, if you ever repeat that outside of this room...."

"Have no fear, Mama, I shall be the definition of discretion should I ever choose to follow that path."

Nothing was said for a great while after that. All that could be heard was the unbearable sound of tea being sipped. Caroline wondered why she would have ever voiced such a scandalous idea to begin with. It was not as though she had any intentions of carrying out the threat, after all.

Especially not if the marriage bed was as horrible as she believed it was going to be.

"I think," Wilhelmina said, breaking the silence, "that you are going to find your marriage surprises you in more ways than you expect."

Caroline stared at her sister.

"What makes you think that?"

"Just a feeling I have." The younger girl grinned. "I also think that you shall be the last to realise it."

"Realise what?"

"Wait and see."

Caroline glanced at her mother, but only saw the same knowing look her sister was giving her. Whatever it was, it had better happen sooner rather than later.

Chapter Seventeen

Lord Duncan Wexford, the most notorious rake in all of London, was a married man.

Married for an approximate eleven hours, that is.

Eleven hours of perhaps the greatest example of self-restraint he had ever exhibited. His first kiss with the woman he had spent recent months lusting after was chaste and not at all what his instincts were screaming at him to be.

He only allowed himself the slightest of touches. Duncan had kept his hand on her arm, in her hand, on the small of her back but only briefly.

Anymore and he was certain Caroline would faint. She had appeared rather pale for the entire ceremony, and he thought he had only seen three or four genuine smiles during the eleven hours she had been his wife.

Now, Duncan had been staring at his reflection in his dressing room for eleven minutes.

He had no intentions of convincing his bride to do anything she did not feel comfortable with. If the unthinkable happened, and she did willingly give him her maidenhead that night, Duncan would use every weapon in his arsenal to make the experience as pleasurable for her as possible.

Of course, Duncan had no expectations of anything more than a little kissing that night. And he intended to savour her kisses.

By the morning, he expected Caroline will have been so thoroughly kissed that she would be a great deal more eager for more than just kisses.

But Duncan would be patient. He cared more for his wife's sensitivities than his own lust. Barely.

His reflection having somehow convinced him that he could go through the night with ease, Duncan put out the candle and ventured through his room to knock on their adjoining door.

Hearing a squeaking voice telling him to enter, he took a deep breath and entered Caroline's domain. A terrifying place indeed.

The only part of her he could see were her arms and face. She was stiff as a board underneath the covers and clinging to them so that they stayed tight up to her neck.

"Is it cold, My Lady?" Duncan chuckled, managing to briefly change her petrified expression to one of ire.

Meandering around the bed, he pulled his shirt over his head and absentmindedly tossed it to the floor. Coming to stand beside the empty bedside, he was about to pull down the covers and climb in when he saw an even more horrified than before look on Caroline's face, if that were possible.

"What?"

"What is that *thing*?" she shrieked.

Wondering what on earth the girl was getting at, Duncan followed her line of sight to see that it was directed on his cock.

His hand rose to rub over his eyes at how he had thoughtlessly removed every article of clothing as was his habit each night.

It was too late to dwell on that now, though, and Duncan simply shrugged at settled into bed. He hid his smirk at how his wife shifted in the bed as far away from him as she could without falling off.

"I thought you said your mother had advised you of all the details of the marriage bed?" he finally answered.

"She did not say that men had a giant monstrosity attached to their person!"

"You think it giant? Now, that is a compliment."

"Trust me, it is not." He could almost hear the scowl on her face.

"Luckily for you, I have every intention of keeping my promise to you and shall not be doing any ravishing tonight, as much as it pains me to say."

With that, he turned to the candle on his bedside table and blew it out. Making himself comfortable, Duncan began to imagine the least arousing thoughts he could fathom to avoid being tempted by the girl lying beside him.

Unfortunately, that was rather difficult when said girl was tossing and turning every five seconds.

Just as he was prepared to say something, she suddenly stilled, and Duncan thought it meant she was finally falling asleep. Instead, he felt the bed suddenly jerk and heard her begin to wander about the room.

The tell-tale sound of candles being lighted reached his ears. Duncan did not open his eyes, though, until he felt the bedcovers being thrust off him.

Caroline stood over him, hands on her hips, staring intently at his appendage. Said appendage was, for some bizarre reason, becoming a little aroused under her unhinged gaze.

"IT MOVED!" she screamed, jumping backwards.

"It tends to do that when in the presence of a beautiful woman." Duncan sighed, bringing his hands up behind his head.

She looked at him suspiciously, shuffling closer to bed. He remained as still as possible, determined not to bring about another outburst from his wife.

Truthfully, Duncan found her reaction to him both amusing and refreshing. He desperately wanted to laugh but knew that would not go down well with Caroline.

She cautiously lowered herself down to perch on the bed beside him. The sight of her tongue peeking out of the corner of her tempting mouth as she inspected him made his mouth go a little dry.

A hand then reached out and Duncan felt a finger lightly brushed over him, causing him to let out a hiss. Her hand did not retreat, but her movements did freeze for a moment.

"Just be gentle." His words came out strangled. As Caroline resumed her movements, his eyes snapped shut.

It was only a single finger exploring his member, but its light touch made him spring to full arousal in no time.

A small gasp left her lips, but her movements did not cease. A second finger then came to join the first's caresses, then a third. Soon enough, her hand was gently clasped around his length and stroking.

A guttural groan left his mouth and Duncan felt the desperate need to thrust into her hand. Instead, he let out small murmurings of advice between moans.

Like a perfect pupil, Caroline sped up, slowed down, stroked, twisted, and pulled at every request. If it were not such a pleasurable experience, he would have been ashamed of how fast it took him to reach his peak.

With a final strangled groan, he could resist no longer, and his hips raised off the bed as he spent himself into her hand.

Giving himself a moment to regain his breath, Duncan kept his eyes clenched shut. After a minute, with continued silence from Caroline, he finally opened them to find his new wife staring at him thoughtfully.

With a grin, he rose to sit up and shifted down to sit beside her. Cupping her face in his hands, he took her mouth in a slow kiss. Determined to both relish the moment and show his thanks for what she had just done.

Brushing his tongue against her lips, he coaxed her to open for him. He tangled it around hers and was delighted to find her mimicking his movements. She was truly turning out to be a perfect pupil.

Unwilling to push her further by exploring her body, Duncan only allowed himself to softly stroke her cheeks with his thumbs.

He had waited longer for Caroline than he had for any other woman before, and he had no intention of rushing her.

Caroline decided that she quite liked Duncan's kisses. He was not being overly forceful like she imagined he might be. He simply coaxed her gently to respond to him. Just as he did when she had touched him.

She shivered at the memory of what had happened just a few minutes before. When she had first seen his…. *thing*, Caroline had been horrified but soon enough the sight of her husband's face as she touched him intoxicated her.

She did not even know what possessed her to get out of bed to examine it more closely, but she had no regrets over doing so.

The look of unadulterated pleasure in his features made her feel a little powerful. In the grip of her hand, she had been able to reduce her constant combatant to a groaning wreck.

She just wished she could know how it felt herself. As she continued to give in to Duncan's kisses, she thought to herself *why should she not know?*

"Duncan." she murmured, practically humming as his lips began to move down her neck. He found a particularly sensitive area to suck on and the jolt of pleasure Caroline felt caused her to let out a squeak.

"Hmmm?" His voice was muffled against her neck.

"Could you…...would you……make me feel the same?"

He froze at her question. His head lifted from its resting place, and he stared at her in wonder.

"Please?" Caroline shyly asked once more.

His lips contorting into a smile, he nodded his head and gently beckoned her to lie back on the bed.

He resumed his kisses and Caroline found her hands moving of their own volition to run through his chestnut locks.

She barely registered his undoing the buttons on the front of her nightgown until she felt his hands cup her bare breasts.

Her mouth opened with a gasp, and he took the opportunity to thrust his tongue inside her with less restraint than before. He began to knead her breasts, causing Caroline to pant. Then, his thumbs moved to stroke her nipples in synchronisation with his hands.

Caroline found herself murmuring indistinguishable words into his mouth as he continued to toy with her stiffened nipples. Her hips began to move in time with the jolts of pleasure as each one shot through her body.

"Oh god!" she cried as she tore her mouth from his. "Please Duncan."

He trailed kisses over her face, down her neck and chest until he took her breast into his mouth, Caroline held onto his head for dear life as her hips bucked more incessantly than before.

She was so focused on how his tongue was now replicating the movements on the thumb remaining on her other breast that she did not notice how his free hand was drifting lower down her body.

Her eyes bulged wide open at the first feel of a finger on her most private area. It trailed up and down her folds, gathering up moisture that had appeared inexplicably.

It came to rest on one particular spot which he kept circling and pressing, increasing her arousal. After a moment of bliss, the finger was replaced by a thumb Whilst the former digit drifted lower until Caroline felt it prodding at her entrance.

She felt overwhelmed by the pleasure from his ministrations on her breasts and quim, but at the same time, the feeling of his finger slowly pushing its way inside her was a little painful.

"Just breathe, darling." she heard Duncan say, and tried to follow his advice, taking deep breaths, and relaxing into his touch.

It helped a little and soon she felt a second finger accompany the first, deliberately thrusting in and out of her. His head left her breast to resume his trail of kisses, this time drifted even lower until his head was level with her quim.

Caroline whined in protest for a moment when his thumb moved away but quickly cried out as his mouth replaced it. Her back arched in ecstasy as he drew the little nub into his mouth and suckled.

As he alternated between sucking and teasing her with his tongue, a third finger entered her and, to Caroline's surprise, she found her hips attempting to move in time with his fingers. Only his free hand holding her down kept her in place.

Both their movements became more frantic, and she was desperately chasing after an unknown goal that constantly loomed just out of her reach.

Drenched in both arousal and sweat, Caroline needed something. She had no clue what though. All she knew was that she needed more and kept crying it out to her husband.

To her distress, he ceased his movements altogether. Moving back up her body, Duncan took her mouth in a needy kiss, which she reciprocated whole heartedly. Tasting herself on her husband's tongue, Caroline could not help but feel a little wanton and scandalous at how it pleased her to know it was from him pleasuring her.

"Caro, can I?" he muttered against her lips. "Will you let me......?" Even if he did not outright say what he was asking for, she knew and she needed it too.

"Yes please." She kissed him then, wrapping her legs around his hips and wantonly grinding herself against him.

Duncan's head rose to hover above her. She felt as if he could not believe what she was agreeing to and nodded her head in confirmation once more.

He nodded back. Their gazes remained locked on one another as she felt him position himself.

"Oh!" she exclaimed in surprise upon feeling his member stroke along her folds before resting against her entrance.

Duncan's head lowered once more. However, he did not kiss her. Instead, his mouth moved to beside her ear.

"Take a deep breath." he whispered, causing her to shiver. She did as he bade. As she was exhaling, he moved, suddenly thrusting fully inside of her. Caroline let out a cry of both pain and surprise.

The only part of him that moved for a great while after that was his mouth. He placed soft, loving kisses on every inch of her he could reach, all the while gently urging her to relax and breathe.

Though she still felt a little uncomfortable, Caroline began to feel it was more bearable having him inside her and uttered small requests for him to begin moving.

He only moved a little at first, allowing her to adjust to each change. One of his hands came to rest beside her head on the pillows as the other moved down to stroke at that little bud of pleasure once more.

He stroked in time with his thrusts and soon she found pleasure mixing with the pain. Hesitantly, Caroline began to match his movements and found herself wanting to do more upon seeing the look of delight on Duncan's face at her actions.

Clasping hold of his shoulders, their movements sped up until Caroline did not think they could possibly go any faster.

Every cry of pleasure she made was matched with his own deeper groan and their lips kept finding one another in desperate need until they had no more breath.

She felt herself tittering on the brink of pleasure, unable to quite push herself over it. So focused on reaching that goal was she, that her brows furrowed in determination.

During one of the moments when their lips had parted, Duncan must have observed the look on her face. For, suddenly, his head fell, and she felt that same spot on her neck from before being covered by his mouth.

It was the final push she needed to go over that brink and Caroline forgot where she was, who she was with, even who she was. All she could she was brightness as the feeling of pure bliss enveloped over every inch of her.

Slowly, she felt herself coming back down to earth. It was then that she realised that Duncan had stopped moving entirely and a strange warmth was inside her.

He must have finished at the same time.

She brought her hands to cup his face and softly urged her husband to kiss her once more. Unlike their earlier kisses, this one was almost lazy as they revelled in their satisfaction with one another.

After what felt like an eternity, Caroline felt herself grow a little stiff, and so gently pushed him off her.

Coming to rest on his back, she saw out of the corner of her eye Duncan's hands running over his face.

She almost laughed at the look of astonishment he bore. As though he could not quite believe what had just occurred.

His eyes moved to rest upon her, and he realised that she had been staring at him. He shook his head, a grin forming on his lips.

"For god's sake, Caroline!" he burst out. "That was not supposed to happen for a least a week."

Bursting into a fit of laughter, Caroline found herself feeling better already and moved to lie on him, already looking forward to their next round of lovemaking.

Chapter Eighteen

Dear lord, the new Mrs Wexford was just as insatiable as Duncan had hoped. He thought he had died and gone to heaven!

Only a single week had passed since they had wed, and he genuinely believed that he had made love more times in that week than any other week in his life.

And with just the one woman!

Not only that, but the belief Duncan had had since that very first carnal thought of Caroline that the novelty would quickly wear off showed no sign of being true at all. If anything, he wanted her more. It was truly an extraordinary turn of events.

It was getting a little in the way of the rest of his life, he had to admit, but he was most certainly not complaining about that. Caroline could disturb him in his study to demand he pleasure her any day of the week. Eleanor of Aquitaine could wait!

In fact, Duncan found it a little annoying when his older brother arrived on his doorstep after seven days of marriage had passed to drag him to Whites.

And he made that feeling very clear.

"Guess what, little brother," Matt responded upon being seated at the club after the fiftieth protest, "I do not care."

Duncan slunk low in his chair, staring daggers at the older man, who laughed.

"Come along, man, we allowed you an entire week before beginning our rescue."

"I am not in need of rescuing." Duncan protested. "And who is we?"

"Who else?" a voice said from behind. The owner punctuated his point by lightly prodding the back of Duncan's head. He was unsurprised to see his younger brother then taking the seat beside his own.

"Oh good, the entire clan is here."

"Is Mama here?" Harry asked with a sly grin.

"If there is one respectable woman who could make her way into a gentleman's club without scandal, it is our mother." Matt responded.

"I think our sister and wives would have something to say about that." A look of realisation crossed the younger man's face then, and he turned back to Duncan. "Good lord, that includes Caroline now, does it not? Yes, in that case, she would be leading the charge."

"I hate you all."

"What is wrong with him?" Harry directed the question to Matt.

"It seems that he is actually enjoying married life."

Both of his brother's sent him teasing looks, angering Duncan once more. He practically barked out the order for a strong drink. He needed it.

"I think," Harry spoke after ordering his own glass, "that my prediction was correct, and Miss Caroline is truly our foolish middle brother's perfect match."

"That is Lady Duncan to you."

"You owe me ten bob." Harry nodded to his eldest brother, ignoring Duncan completely.

He watched, incredulous, as Matt casually took the money out of his pocket and passed it to their younger brother.

"I thought you considered Caroline and I the perfect match?" he exclaimed.

"I did." Matt replied. "I still do. I just thought the pair of you were too stubborn to realise it this soon."

"I never said I thought Caroline was perfect for me! I am simply enjoying being married to a dear friend."

"*Friend.*" Harry smirked. Duncan resisted the urge to hurl a cushion at him.

"Have the pair of you any news from this past week?" he asked, changing the subject.

"You mean whilst you were busy with your *friend?*"

"Shut up!" Duncan barked at his younger brother. He sent a pleading look to Matt, who rolled his eyes.

"Nothing of interest." he answered. "Have you really paid no heed to the world outside your house this week?"

Duncan's jaw clenched in annoyance. It seemed there was no possible hope that he would avoid this conversation. Especially if Matt were involved. Harry he could swat away like a fly at least.

"Do we have to do this? Surely my marriage is not the business of either of you?"

"Did you hear that, big brother?" Harry grinned. "Our brother's marriage is none of our business."

"Very interesting." Matt nodded, his expression thoughtful. "Of course, one would assume that he has regarded our marriages the same way."

"Undoubtably. A man with that attitude must have left our marriages to themselves, must he not?"

"I hate the both of you."

"How long do you suppose we torture him for?" Matt smirked to their younger brother.

"Whenever the occasion calls for it, surely." came Harry's reply. "I have waited too long to have my revenge."

"You have only been married for two years!" Duncan cried.

"But I have been your brother for three and twenty. One must take those years into account."

Duncan had never been more relieved than when his drink arrived. Before he had even taken the first sip of his brandy, he requested another two.

"In all seriousness," Matt appeared earnest at last, "we all simply wish you to be happy. I trust that you are?"

Duncan looked between his brothers, unsure as to how much he should reveal to them. In all honesty, he knew that what he was feeling for Caroline was much deeper than he could have imagined.

He was not in love with the woman, at least not yet, but he could see a clear path towards those feelings. The lust and friendship they had already shared increased tenfold, and he could not imagine a life where he was not wed to Caroline.

In fact, in the back of his mind, Duncan was kicking himself for not realising sooner how perfect of a match she was. If he had only known, he would have properly courted her at the beginning of the season or would have even travelled to Suffolk before she had even debuted.

Deciding that no one needed to hear those musings, Duncan opted for a half-truth.

"I think that, during this past week, I have realised precisely how much my friendship with my wife has meant to me. I cannot foresee any circumstance where I would ever come home with a feeling of dread at what awaited me."

He did not fail to notice the knowing smile on his younger brother's face at his words, nor the thoughtful look on that of his elder brother.

"I am not a fool," he continued, "and do not believe my marriage shall ever have the type of love and affection that your own have. But it has a comfort and a strong foundation that makes me just as happy."

To that last part, Duncan could not deny that it was true. No matter what feelings he bore for his wife, she did not feel the same. But she regarded him as one of her closest of friends and confidants, and she was attracted to him. That was enough.

"Do not rule it out too soon, Duncan." Matt advised. "You have more than Jane and I ever had when we first wed and look at us now."

Duncan slowly nodded, thinking over his brother's words.

It was true. Matt and Jane had been attracted to one another, but his brother's stubbornness had meant their marriage had gone on for years with no affection whatsoever. It was only when Matt decided that he needed an heir that he and his wife had even begun to fall in love.

But he and Caroline were not Matt and Jane. Nor were they Harry and Eliza. As hard as it was to believe, Duncan would have it no other way.

"Perhaps," he responded, "but my wife and I will always be great friends. I think I prefer that than the uncertainty of love."

"Whenever two humans are involved, there will be uncertainty." Harry argued.

Duncan inclined his head to the man, He hated it when Harry was right!

"Are we going to spend the entire day talking about me?" he asked, receiving two nods in answer.

"We must have some excitement," replied Harry, "the pair of us are stuck at home with wives and children. You are the only source of entertainment we have."

"You say that, but I can guarantee that if I ask you how Patrick or Verity are, you will begin to animatedly regale the current goings on in your nursery."

To that, Matt opened his mouth to speak, but Duncan gave him no chance. "As would you if I were to enquire after little Edmund."

"Just think," Matt grinned, "you have all this to come, brother."

"Even better, he has to do it all with Caroline."

"You just wait! My wife shall put the rest of the family to shame with her maternal instincts."

"The only thing I should give her, it that she already has a little experience owing to her brother being eleven years her junior."

"See, Matthew, you have proven my point." Duncan pointed a finger at his older brother. "She already has the experience."

"Are we to assume that there shall be no nanny's or governesses in your employ, then?" Duncan shook his head at Harry's question.

"Nonsense! Who else should look after the child when we go visiting to rub our victory in?"

"Yes, yes. You will be gloating until the cows come home, but hear this, little brother. You can harp on about how easy it will all be now, but just wait until theory becomes reality."

"What of it?"

Matt looked from Duncan to Harry and back to Duncan again, all the while having the widest grin on his face.

"Say what you want about us," he answered, "but we do not have to deal with the progeny of you and Caroline."

It was entirely unintentional, but Duncan's first instinct upon hearing his brother's words was to wince. Naturally, the other two Wexford men burst into resounding laughter in response.

Duncan gave up at last. He was not going to make it through their time at the club unscathed and decided he might as well allow the men their fun.

After all, the next time they all met as a family, he would have his partner in crime with him, and his brothers would rue the day they had dared go up against Lord and Lady Duncan Wexford.

As such, he played his part for the rest of his meeting, trying to turn the topic back on them and failing at every turn. By the time they left, both Matt and Harry were looking particularly smug with themselves.

Although he did not show it, Duncan also felt a little smug. Primarily because he was about to be rid of them and could go home to his wife.

Of course, Matt sought to irritate him further by demanding the carriage take the scenic route to Duncan's home. Still, he smiled and played along, the only sign of his annoyance being the tight grip he held onto his hat.

Finally arriving home, Duncan practically leapt out of the carriage with barely a word said to his brother. Charging into the house, he enquired as to the whereabouts of his wife and, upon being informed that she was in the parlour, practically ran to the room.

Opening the door wide, their eyes met, and Duncan knew exactly what she wanted. As he hastily slammed the door shut and shed himself of his jacket, he heard her say, "What took you so long?"

Chapter Nineteen

Duncan's head tilted to the side thoughtfully as he examined the sight before him. He was certain there was something off but could not put his finger on what it was.

"You have been staring at this painting for at least ten minutes."

Duncan jumped at his father's voice, fortunate to avoid letting out a shriek on this occasion. He quickly returned to his senses, though.

"Have I?" he asked. The landscape before him had captured his attention not long after arriving at the Royal Academy of Art's exhibition. Caroline had almost immediately left his side to join her mother and sister, the traitor! But he did not think he had been staring at the painting for that long.

After all, how long can someone look at a painting of a simple countryside bridge!

"I thought you were a statue at first." his father replied with a smile.

"If it would prevent me from having to partake in tedious pleasantries with bores, I would gladly be one."

"Who are you and what have you done with my son?" Duncan only shook his head at his father's joke, and the pair casually strode alongside the wall, making odd comments on the art as they saw fit.

"Just so you know," the Duke started, "your mother is planning a family dinner for next week. The attendance of yourself and your wife is required."

"I can only imagine what Mama has planned. No doubt she will burst into tears at how all her children are now happily wed."

"Are they?"

Duncan looked at his father, who was studying him most seriously.

"Are you privy to some gossip involving one of your other son's marriages?"

"You know what I meant." the older man scolded. "And does your sister not count in your mind?"

"If Connie were having any sort of troubles, I would be the first to know."

"You still have not answered my question."

"One day, Papa, you are going to realise that you do not need to know about every detail of your children's lives."

The Duke sighed. "Trust me, I have no desire to discover all that goes on in your life." At that part, the man wrinkled his nose in disgust. "All I wish to know is that my children are all happy."

"Yes, I am. Is that satisfactory?"

"No."

Duncan smirked at his father's blunt reply. He knew he would get off that easily, but until he himself understood precisely what he felt for his wife and if their marriage as it currently stood would satisfy him in the long run, he did not wish to share his feelings with anyone.

"Listen, son," his father spoke before Duncan had the chance, "I understand that you prefer to keep anything above the superficial to yourself, but you are married now. Caroline is not one of your conquests whom you can finish with and come to us with all the juicy details."

"Do you think I do not know that?"

"I think you are in a territory that is largely unfamiliar to you." The Duke came to a halt in his steps, turning to face his son fully. "If not me, then talk to one of your brothers. You are surrounded by happy marriages. Marriages that began in all sorts of ways. Take advantage of that knowledge."

He frowned at his father. "You forget that those very marriages have one fundamental aspect that my own does not."

The older man closed his eyes for a moment, and Duncan felt a little guilty over the rejection, but he knew that there was no use in what was being offered.

"You do not have to always be the smart one, you know." The man's voice sounded rather resigned as he replied, and then he quickly excused himself to go rejoin his wife.

Duncan watched after his father's retreating form. He could not resist smiling upon seeing his mother's eyes light up the moment she spotted her approaching husband.

There was nothing more he wanted than to see that look in his own wife's eyes. He shook his head at the thought. He already had fondness, friendship, and lust from her, why jeopardise that by asking for more?

Besides, it was not as though his father or brothers could help him in that subject, they had never been in the predicament of unrequited love.

The realisation hit Duncan then and there. He was already in love with the woman! Only for Duncan Wexford would the knowledge of being in love with his own wife being positively frustrating.

"I wonder what flitted through that wonderful mind of yours, to cause such a face." a husky voice interrupted his musings.

Duncan turned to face the owner: Grace Montgomery.

The raven-haired beauty had made her debut the same year as Connie and married Rupert Montgomery, a man thrice her age, the following year.

Rumour has it that old Mr Montgomery had been unable to perform for his nubile young wife, causing her to turn elsewhere for satisfaction. Duncan was one of the 'elsewheres'.

Not that they had the chance for anything to happen. The flirtation began a handful of days before Caroline had turned up on his doorstep and so the pair never had the chance to turn words into actions.

In all truth, he had forgotten entirely about the woman. He now felt very awkward, indeed.

"Mrs Montgomery," he bowed, "I can assure you, that it was nothing of interest at all."

"Now, that makes it all the more interesting." She batted her eyelashes at him. "I can only imagine what it could have been."

"Then you shall have to resign yourself to being left in suspense, for a gentleman never tells." He hoped that she would spot the double meaning in his words and realise that he had no intention of following through on their flirtations now.

"I am sure I can tempt it out of you somehow." No such luck, it seemed. "One just needs to know a time and place."

Duncan gulped, hoping his horror and cowardice were not apparent on his face.

"Time and place?" he spluttered out, causing her to blink in confusion for a moment. Unsurprising, Duncan thought, as he doubted that he had ever been so out of sorts when in the company of any lady other than his wife.

Her look of confusion quickly transformed into one of amusement, and she burst into flirtatious laughter.

"Now now, Lord Duncan," a finger trailed over his hand as she spoke, "you must not tease me so for I have been in anticipation for far too long."

"Mrs Montgomery, you must understand…....."

"There you are!"

Duncan started at the sound of his wife's voice and snatched his hand away. A glance at the woman at his side informed him that she was entirely unaffected by Caroline's sudden appearance.

"Caroline!" he exclaimed, moving to stand closer to her. "Might I introduce to you Mrs Rupert Montgomery." Caroline's bemused face turned to the other woman, who curtseyed to her.

"It is an honour, Lady Duncan."

"The honour is mine." Caroline gracefully responded, taking hold of Duncan's arm as she did so. "I do hope that my husband was not boring you to death."

"Quite the opposite." She sent him a coy smile as she answered.

Duncan felt the sudden need to pull on his collar, for it had become rather stifling in the room.

"As much as it pains me to cut our meeting short, I can see my husband calling after me." He inwardly sighed in relief.

"Mrs Montgomery, I hope to meet you again." Even unwittingly, Caroline was able to irritate Duncan.

"And I you. If you will excuse me." She curtseyed once more before sauntering away. Duncan offered a pained smile in goodbye, which she somehow took as seductive, judging by her immediate expression afterwards.

He would need to practice his faces in the mirror sometime.

"It is awfully warm in here, do you not think?" he asked, giving into the urge to finally tug on the collar.

"Hmmm?" his wife absentmindedly replied. Turning to look at her, Duncan found her staring at Mrs Montgomery in bemusement.

Glancing around to ensure that no one was looking, he drew Caroline's attention back to him with a light pinch upon her derriere. The trademark Caroline squeak that ensued was music to his ears.

"What was that for?" she scolded.

"Did no one ever tell you it is rude to stare?" he retorted back.

"I was just wondering who her husband was," she glanced back again, "she went to join her grandfather instead."

"That is her husband." Duncan gritted out.

Caroline's eyes widened, and she glanced back at the pair several more times before she could formulate a sentence.

"How old is he?"

"None of your business."

"Fine." Duncan wanted to kiss that pout off her face. Alas, even his reputation could not withstand that. Instead, he settled for covering her hand with his.

They began to walk along the gallery, but he paid little attention to the paintings before him. Instead, he attempted to prepare a speech for the next time he was confronted by a woman intended on a liaison.

"Duncan."

He turned back to the woman at his side, finding her staring up at him in curiosity.

"Yes, darling?"

"What were you discussing with Mrs Montgomery before I interrupted you?"

It took him a moment to find an answer that would satisfy his wife enough.

"She was asking after Connie. They debuted the same year, you see."

"Why would she ask you when Connie is here? She could just ask her in person."

Bugger!

Caroline frowned at him for a beat, then her eyes widened, and he knew she had caught on.

"Oh gosh!" she smirked. "Did I interrupt something scandalous? We must come up with some sort of signal, so that I know not to interrupt. Or should I just stay away if I see you talking to a beautiful woman?"

"Caroline…..."

"Then again, I suppose it is not always outward beauty that should attract you, or is my husband really that shallow?"

"Stop it."

"You know if you ever need help then I shall be glad to assist. I do not know how but I am sure I could do something. After all, you have a reputation to maintain."

"I swear to God…..."

"Now, you must remember, husband dear, that I am so willing to help in this matter, and I shall do all that I can.

You never know if our positions shall be reversed, and I will need to call upon you for resistance one day."

Duncan froze in his step, horrified at what he had heard. Ice ran through his veins at the mere thought of Caroline with another man.

Before he could start a jealous, possessive rant at her, she caught sight of Connie and moved to join her, leaving Duncan remaining on his spot afraid that if he moved, someone would end up hurt.

Duncan would not have been surprised if he was told steam was coming from his nose.

"What is wrong with you?" Jane asked, having sidled up beside him at some point.

"I have just been propositioned." he bluntly replied.

"Oh," Jane said in a resigned tone, "that has a habit of happening to Wexfords at exhibitions."

Brought out of his angry reverie, Duncan turned to ask his sister-in-law's meaning, but she had already wandered off to greet some fellow ladies.

"Why do people keep leaving before the conversation ends?" he barked out loud, earning a handful of perplexed looks.

Giving up on everything, he stormed off in search of his younger brother. With any luck, Harry would have a flask of something hard on his person.

Chapter Twenty

"Lord Henry Wexford is waiting in the entrance hall, My Lady."

Caroline stared, frozen in surprise at Stocks, not quite sure how she felt about the butler's announcement.

She had seen Harry since her wedding, naturally, but only in company. In fact, she could not recall a time where they had ever been truly alone with one another.

Setting down her needlework, she calmly told Stocks to show the man in and to arrange for tea and sandwiches to be sent up.

As Caroline waited, she took several deep breaths, preparing herself to greet the man she had spent half her life in love with.

"Miss Caroline!" he exclaimed as he walked through the door. Caroline rose from her chair, feeling her heart skip a beat at his charming smile.

"Harry, what a delightful surprise." She masked her lovestruck feelings for the man with surprising ease. "Although my husband is busy in his study, writing currently.

I can send for him if you wish. I should not delude myself that I am the one you have come to visit."

"Nonsense! Dunc is only a minor reason to visit this house. You are better company by far."

She found herself needing to retake her seat, suddenly weak at the knees. Harry took his hostess' lead, lowering himself into the chair beside hers and setting his cane to the side.

"How is married life treating you?" he started. "I assume Duncan is boring you already."

"Not at all. Surprisingly he suits married life quite well." Caroline narrowed her eyes in mischief then. "But please never tell him I said that. We should not wish for his head to get any bigger than it already is."

Harry burst into musical laughter at that. "Never!"

"I would not expect any less of you." She felt herself beaming without even realising it. That troubled her. Less than a minute with Harry Wexford and Caroline was already getting the same feelings she had born for so many years.

She had to hide the threatening frown. She was so happy with Duncan, but the man sat beside her was causing Caroline to second guess herself.

Harry, to his credit, did not let on if he noticed her slight change in demeanour. His expression, however, did turn a little more serious.

"You know, I am awfully happy that you are now part of the family. I cannot think of anyone more suited to joining our ranks."

"You are simply saying that to be polite, Captain."

Harry put his hand over his heart in response. "I am being entirely serious. Of all the 'married-ins', you are the one who I had no doubts about fitting in from the first. And I have told you before to call me Harry."

Warmth spread over Caroline's entire being at that. Surely his placing her before his own wife in that declaration was a sign of his true feelings.

"I still do not believe you." She could not hide her smile as she responded. "Besides, have I not always been a member of the family?"

"Yes, but the stepdaughter of my cousin is not quite the same as the wife of my brother." he argued. "This way, we are all more closely related than before and the closer the relation, the more often we can all see each other."

He wished to see her more often! If she did not know Harry to be a noble man, she would have sworn he was practically offering himself for a lover.

"We shall be sick of each other within the week." Caroline was pleased to see her answer amused him.

"You underestimate my tolerance, Caroline dear." That set off the butterflies in her stomach. "I lived with your husband for nigh on twenty years, how neither of us are seriously maimed, I do not know."

Caroline could not help the brief glance downwards. Harry spotted it and the pair quickly burst into laughter.

"From each other, then." he corrected himself. "In any case, I know what it is like to have to live with my beast of a brother. Should you ever find yourself in need of an escape, I shall be more than willing to help."

Willing herself not to cry, Caroline strived to maintain a light-hearted airiness.

"Watch out," she managed to get out, "or it shall be Duncan on your doorstep instead."

"Part of me supposes that you should wish for me to suffer. What did I ever do to you?"

Marry someone else.

"Nothing." Caroline said instead of revealing her true thoughts. "I just think that, should my husband irritate me that much, then he should be the one to leave."

Harry's examining gaze on her was thoughtful, and he began to nod slightly in approval.

"Quite right."

By that point, the tea had finally arrived, and Caroline's cheeks turned pink when her guest exclaimed his approval of the sandwiches. As she began to pour them both drinks, he practically shoved two of the foodstuffs into his mouth.

"Pardon my lack of manners," he swallowed the last bite, "but I skipped breakfast this morning and find myself utterly famished."

"Why would you do such a foolish thing?"

"The even worse older brother sent for me first thing. I swear, Liza practically shoved me out of bed so she could go back to sleep." His face became rather serious, and Caroline let out a small gasp when he took her hands in his. "Promise me you will never do the same."

Caroline was silent for a moment, staring at his earnest face in disbelief. He meant Duncan, she told herself, he is asking you to be kind to his brother.

Thinking on it, Caroline could not believe she would ever do so to her husband anyway. Now that they were wed, she found him annoying her less and less each day.

But the way Harry was looking at her now, and how she felt her heart flutter in his presence, confused her very much indeed.

Duncan wanted to crawl into a hole and die.

He had been proud of himself, having finally finished the first draft of his book, and wanted to share his happiness with his wife.

When he had passed Stocks and been told that his younger brother was calling, he had thought nothing of it other than a slight irritation that he had to behave with more propriety that he would have liked with Caroline.

The sight that greeted him when he arrived at the open doorway to the morning room had the same effect as a cold bucket of water being poured over him.

Duncan had only realised his true feelings for his wife three days prior. Since then, he had decided it was entirely possible that she could reciprocate his love. After all, he had thought, she gave every indication when they were together that she was utterly happy.

But the way she was looking at Harry made it all come crashing down, and Duncan was back to reality.

He had thought it was just a childish infatuation that she was over. Yes, she blushed when he teased her about it, but no one actually believed that she bore anything stronger than that. But here it was, clear as day!

Caroline was in love with his brother.

His heart tore in two at the way her eyes glistened as she gazed at him. She never looked at Duncan that way!

Devastation turned to jealous rage, however, when his ignoramus of a brother had the gall to take her hands in his. They stared at one another for a moment and Duncan decided that he could take no more.

"Am I interrupting something?" he asked, keeping his voice calm and his face neutral so to not give his thoughts and feelings away.

Harry, unsurprisingly, fell back in his seat, finally releasing her hands, as he warmly offered a greeting. Caroline, on the other hand, had a brief flash of guilt on her face, which she quickly masked.

"It is about time you arrived," the younger man said, picking up a teacup, "I was on the verge of boring your sweet wife to tears with my ramblings."

As annoyed as Duncan was at the entire scene before him, he knew that his brother was entirely innocent, and refused to do anything that would bring him into it.

"I do not recall ever hearing my wife described as sweet." That took the meek look off the woman's face at least.

"That is because you are the one person whom I refuse to be sweet to." Caroline scowled, making both men laugh.

Duncan joined the pair for tea, appearing as innocent as it was possible for him to be. All the while, however, he watched the pair like a hawk.

From the chaise opposite them, chosen deliberately for its vantage point, obviously, he saw nothing untoward in his brother's behaviour. Harry was simply being his charming, carefree self, as irritating as that was.

Caroline, on the other hand, was putting on a front obvious to all those who looked for it. Her looks on the younger man lasted a second too long, she deferred to his opinion over her own husbands, and she blushed at every glance or compliment he sent her way.

Even her body was angled towards him.

Nothing relieved Duncan more than when his brother set down his cup and proclaimed that it was time for him to leave. Rising to his feet, Duncan said that he would walk the younger man out.

The unreasonable part of him wanted to ensure that the man had undeniably departed the building, especially when the irritant kissed his wife's hand as goodbye.

Duncan had to stop himself pulling his brother's arm from its socket to get him out.

"Marriage seems to agree with your wife very much." Harry commented as soon as they were out of earshot of the morning room.

Yes, it does! Because I make her happy, not you. I bring MY WIFE to release multiple times every night. Something you could not do, you incapable buffoon!

"You think so?" Duncan answered calmly.

"Yes, and what is more," Harry sent him a meaningful look, "I think it agrees with you also."

"What was in your tea?" Duncan joked as they arrived at the door.

"Believe it or not, big brother, I do actually wish to see you happy." Harry pulled him in to a surprising hug as he spoke. "Even if you do not agree with the rest of us, you really do seem to have found your perfect person."

Without another word, Harry retrieved his hat and gloves from the footman and walked out the door, leaving Duncan staring open-mouthed until his brother finally left his sight.

"Drat!" Duncan burst out, startling a passing maid. His brother really was wonderful, of course Caroline was in love with him!

With that thought, Duncan's feelings of jealousy now returned in full force. Only this time, he could do something about it.

Practically storming back to the morning room, he ignored whatever comment Caroline made about his brother and tossed her needlework to the side.

"Duncan! Whatever do you think you are doing?"

She offered no more protests, however, as Duncan did not wait a moment more before falling to his knees and pulling her skirts up. Dragging his wife to the edge of her seat, his head shot between her legs, and he began to relentlessly feast upon her quim.

Her startled gasp was soon followed by moans of pleasure, and Duncan smiled to himself when her hands ran through his hair and pulled him closer to her.

Focusing his tongue on her little bud of pleasure, he was rewarded by the taste of her arousal and his ministrations were soon conducted with no friction at all.

With one final lick, he decided Caroline was ready and he pulled his unprotesting wife onto the floor. Positioning her onto her hands and knees, he knelt behind her as he hurriedly untied his breeches and pulled his hard cock out.

Without a moment's hesitation, Duncan sheathed himself inside her and began to thrust with more urgency than ever before.

He knew that he would not last long, and a small part of him wanted to punish her for her feelings by taking his own pleasure whilst leaving her lingering on the edge with no such release in sight.

His pride refused to do so, however, and Duncan's hand fell beneath her as he expertly toyed with her the way he knew drove her to abandon.

In no time at all, he felt the pulsating squeeze of Caroline reaching her peak, and the feeling, as it always did, caused him to follow after her.

Lacking the strength to hold them both up any longer, Duncan collapsed to his side. Out of the corner of his eye, he could see his wife had fallen to lie flat on the floor.

"Oh gosh!" she exclaimed, burying her head in her hands.

"What is it?" Duncan asked through staggered breath.

"You left the door open." Caroline could not have sounded more horrified if she tried.

Duncan felt a little guilty but as soon as she lifted her head to reveal her mortified face, he could not help but laugh.

Moving over to her, he rolled his wife onto her back and covered her body with his. Taking her mouth in a tender kiss, Duncan tried to convince himself that this was enough for the both of them.

It did not work.

Chapter Twenty-One

Caroline felt as though she had joined the most exclusive club in London. It was the first Wexford family dinner she had ever attended and, for the first time in her life, she did not know quite what to say.

The fact that she was so out of sorts was utterly ridiculous. She had known the majority of those present for a decade. Somehow, that did not make her feel less like she had been pushed into the lion's den.

The Duchess had even decided to give Caroline the highest honour of being seated to the right of the Duke himself!

The fact that Harry was sat to her own right added to her ill-ease even more. How on earth was she supposed to behave as though there was nothing amiss between the pair of them when her husband and his wife sat only a few seats away?

Closer than that even, for Duncan had been placed directly across from Harry! Reflecting upon her confusion for the past two days, she could not help but use her vantage point to compare the two brothers.

Surprisingly, little had changed from their younger years, with their identical chestnut locks and emerald eyes. But where the younger brother was lean and youthful, her husband possessed a little fat, and his looks were more mature.

But there was something in their demeanours that she could not help but notice. Both appeared to be totally at ease in the presence of their family but there was something a little less natural about it for Duncan.

Trying not to stare at her husband for too long, Caroline was certain there was something a little tense or unsure in his manner. Something that she was not used to seeing with him.

It confused her very much, for he had appeared so very happy when they were alone together, and she could not complain about their marriage at all. She had never felt so happy and at ease in her life.

But tonight, something was different. Perhaps it was because it was her first meal as his wife with his family and he was worried for her? Perhaps he saw her nervousness?

Whatever it was, her presence at the dinner was affecting him, and she could not help but feel touched at the fact. It was yet another reason for Caroline to be grateful for her marriage.

If only her brother-in-law's presence did not distract her from her happiness whenever they met, then all would be perfect.

In her musings, Caroline had failed to see that her hostess had risen from her chair to signal the ladies that it was time to depart from the table.

"Allow me to assist you, Caroline." the Duke said, laying a hand on her chair and gaining the girl's attention.

It took her a moment to realise what was going on, but Caroline soon caught up and stood, graciously thanking her host as she did so.

Still quiet, she followed the chattering ladies into the drawing room, where she took a seat on one of the chaise's and half-heartedly listened to the conversation around her.

She almost jumped when a voice suddenly whispered in her ear.

"We are not that scary, are we?"

Caroline turned to the owner and found that the space beside her was being occupied by Eliza. She had to swallow the lump of terror in her throat.

"It strikes me," Eliza went on, "that the two of us should be a great deal more acquainted than we currently are."

"Really?" Caroline squeaked out.

"Do you not think so? I thought it rather obvious given our circumstances."

"What circumstances are those?" Caroline asked, befuddled.

"That we are related three times over." Eliza appeared amused. "If that does not warrant a closer relationship, I do not know what does."

Caroline nodded in understanding. It was interesting, she had to admit, that Eliza was both her stepfather's sister, her husband's brother's wife, and her mother's cousin's wife.

"You would think that there was some mystical force connecting our families together."

"I keep being surprised by it, in all truth." Eliza admitted. "I had always thought that Harry and I were the beginning of it all, and Connie marrying one of my brother's closest friends was a simple coincidence."

"Then my Mama went and added to your confusion." The golden-haired woman's eyes widened at that, as though she was remembering some scandalous event of her past, which Caroline supposed she was.

"I was positively gobsmacked when Liam announced he was engaged. None to mention how he had been in love with her for ten or so years."

"Imagine how my sister and I felt!" Caroline exclaimed. "We were expecting this season to go smoothly with one of us hopefully wed by the end. Next thing we know, Mama is the first to do so to a man we had never even met before."

"If I were you, I would have been furious. I can only imagine how I would feel now if my mother did the same." Eliza unexpectedly took Caroline's hand in her own. "But you must know that, in spite of how this all began, my brother really thinks the world of you and your siblings."

Caroline smiled at that. "I must confess, I tried my utmost to dislike him when we first met, but Liam has the uncanny ability to win you over."

"Only when he has reason to." The other woman pursed her lips in thought. "You do not happen to have any other Wexford relatives of marriageable age, do you?"

Caroline thought for a moment, then shook her head. "None close enough that I can think of."

"Well, if another Wexford appears out of nowhere and up and weds one of my remaining siblings, I shall have to turn to the occult. For there can be no other explanation."

It was completely unintentional, but Caroline found herself laughing at that comment. Not only laughing but agreeing with the woman!

She was becoming even more conflicted by the minute. First, she was happy with Duncan. Then, whenever Harry popped up, her prior feelings for the man reappeared.

Now, she was finding herself liking Eliza more and more, and thought that they had the potential to be quite good friends.

What the heavens was going on?

Caroline did not have much time to reflect on this realisation, however, as the men appeared striding through the door, seemingly all in good spirits.

"What is going on here?" Connie teased as her husband kissed her cheek. "Are you all really that attached that you cannot last five minutes without your wives?"

"Blame our middle brother," Harry winked at his sister, "he is still in the stage of besotted newlywed bliss."

He punctuated his point with another wink, this time directed at Caroline, who blushed furiously. She had to ensure that no eye contact was made with the man, as Duncan had decided at that moment to perch on the side of the chaise beside her. One glance told her that he was decidedly unamused.

"Or could it possibly be, little brother, that I find your fiftieth recounting of antics you got up to half a decade ago to be somewhat tedious."

"You should try being married to him." Eliza quipped.

"I cannot think of a more horrifying prospect."

"I am sure when you come to trial for my murder, Duncan will provide an excellent character reference." Harry said, coming to sit beside his wife.

Connie's husband, the Earl, chuckled at that. "As someone who has had the misfortune of your wife's company for longer than you have, I find it surprising that you believe she would be caught."

"Let us face it," Duncan said, "when Harry is inevitably murdered, it shall be a joint effort on all our parts."

Harry put his hand to his chest in mock horror. "Betrayed by my own family! Caroline, can you believe what your husband is saying? You would not think to conspire with him, would you?"

Oh god!

Caroline's gaze darted back and forth between the two men, entirely unsure of what to say. In the end, a small "of course not" left her lips. Whilst her brother-in-law declared himself victorious, she did not fail to note the tightening of her husband's jaw. Perhaps she chose wrong?

"What is happening?" Matt burst out. "I thought we had already agreed that Duncan would be the one to drive us to commit murder?"

"Sometimes your brother deserves the night off." Caroline was surprised by Cora's teasing remark and could not resist laughing at the wicked smirk that appeared on the woman's face.

"If we are returning to topic back to Duncan being offed," Connie started, "the question I have is whether his wife will assist in the slaughter."

"Is that even really a question?" Matt wondered.

Caroline, this time, was far more confident in her answer and her voice was loud and clear as she made it known.

"Why should I ever wish to get rid of my husband? I refuse to lose such a perfect sparring partner."

The knowing looks shared between the rest of the party meant very little to Caroline. The wide smile on her husband's face, on the other hand, she found infectious, and she gazed back at him with the same joy.

"What sort of magic do the Morton women possess?" Caroline torn her gaze from her husband to the Earl, who had his head tilted towards her.

"Whatever do you mean?" she asked.

"Your mother has turned one of my oldest friends into a smitten dolt, and it looks as though you are very close to doing the same with Duncan here. What is your secret?"

Her cheeks reddened again.

"Smitten is not in my vocabulary." she heard her husband protest. "I am simply happily married. I thought you of all people would know that."

Caroline was certain she was now as red as a tomato. That did not stop her from being delighted at hearing Duncan make such a declaration.

If she had been told that she would feel that way only a few months ago, Caroline would have keeled over in laughter.

"Duncan? Happily married?" the Duke contributed. "I still do not know how we ended up here."

"It is quite obvious. My wife was smarter than the rest of you and thought to trap me into marriage."

"I would say that I am disappointed I did not think of it sooner," his mother answered, "but then we probably would not have dear Caroline here."

"Can you imagine it?" Harry asked. "I can guarantee you would have found a sickening, insipid little debutante to bore us all."

"Why do I feel as though I should take offence at that?" Jane replied.

"I suppose that after six years of marriage, it is about time you are mocked like the rest of us." Matt reassured his wife.

"How have I already been the subject of many Wexford jests after only a fraction of that time, then?" Eliza wondered.

"Because, dear sister," Duncan answered, "you are an Ainsworth. It is in our blood to ruthlessly mock you."

"I wonder what if the cause of my teasing, then?" came the Earl's turn.

"You are practically an Ainsworth. In fact, given her mother's marriage, so is my wife." At that, Duncan leant down to whisper in Caroline's ear. "Sorry darling, but my teasing's must increase tenfold now."

"It is quite alright." she murmured back to him. "I am sure I know the perfect way to punish you when we return home."

"That sounds positively delicious."

"Really? I had no idea you were so keen to sleep in your own bed!"

Duncan's head lifted back as he examined her face. Caroline strived to keep her expression defiant, promising to carry out her threat.

A few moments later, he broke their eye contact.

"Well played."

His response was defeated, and Caroline turned back to the rest of the family feeling rather victorious. Small conversations had developed around them, and she could not help but notice how each of them were accompanied by glances in their direction.

Chapter Twenty-Two

"Come along, Caro. Are you really not going to tell us anything?"

Caroline shook her head at her sister, who poked her tongue out at her in protest.

"Boo!" she whined. "What use is it having a sister married to the most infamous lover in London if she is not willing to give at least some details about it."

It was the first time Caroline had hosted her mother and sister in her new home, and the fact that it was the first time they had met privately since her wedding was being taken advantage of by Wilhelmina.

"I suppose that, if your positions were reversed, you would reveal every piece of information you knew?" Anne surmised, prompting her younger daughter to furiously nod her head in agreement.

"Of course I would! I could not resist gloating over the fact."

"As we have discovered from your many declarations about your own marriage." Caroline teased.

"You cannot blame me for wanting to shout from the rooftops what a wonderful husband I have."

"Does that mean that, because your sister and I do not wish to reveal quite as much information, our husband's pale in comparison?"

"All men pale in comparison to my Ernest," Wilhelmina proclaimed, "although I am biased in the matter."

"Just a little." Caroline spoke after taking a sip of tea. Her sister stared at her, letting out an exaggerated breath.

"Will you tell me something, at least? Life cannot be that dull that you have nothing to share."

"I find there is plenty of excitement that Duncan and I share. The only problem is that you already know of half of it because we have known him for years."

"Yes, but there is a difference between knowing someone and *knowing* them." The younger girl wiggled her eyebrows at her sister.

"Your sister does have a point there." their Mama said to Caroline.

"Oh, you traitor!"

"It is true. Marriage brings out an entire new side of a person never seen before. I can see it already with you."

Caroline was taken aback by that.

"Me? I am not any different at all."

"You are still delusional, at the least then." Wilhelmina earned a filthy look from her sister for that.

"Trust me, as your mother I should know."

"But how? I still feel very much the same old Caroline."

"It is more your demeanour that has changed." Anne explained. "You are somewhat calmer, more settled."

Caroline took a moment to ponder her mother's words.

"I suppose I feel more comfortable as a married woman."

"That is it!" her sister exclaimed. "I felt the same. Once you are married, you no longer have that pressure on you."

"What pressure?"

"To find a husband, silly. For our entire lives, it has been drilled into us that we must find one as soon as we come of age to secure our futures."

"I never felt worried about finding a husband." Caroline disagreed.

"I think your constant protestations to the quality of men contradict that argument, dear."

"That is different." Caroline argued her mother's point. "I wanted to wed but did not find anyone up to scratch. I never thought it was life or death."

"Two weeks married to the historian, and she is already rewriting history." Now it was Caroline's turn to poke her tongue out at her sister.

"Regardless," Wilhelmina went on, "even that argument is proof enough. You did not think anyone was up to scratch, then marriage to Duncan changed that. Simply because the two of you are so well suited."

"Because we enjoy teasing one another?"

"I do believe that teasing helps in other areas as well." Caroline ignored that suggestion, even if it was somewhat true.

Nonetheless, she had no intention of revealing anything about the activities she and Duncan got up to once they went to bed……or any other time of day.

"Perhaps we should venture onto another topic?" Anne suggested. "Any other topic."

"Yes, lets." Wilhelmina agreed a little too enthusiastically for her sister's taste.

"Yes, is there any sign of a new little brother or sister yet?" she asked her mother, determined to prevent whatever was on her sister's mind from being said.

Anne's eyes widened in horror and a flush creeped up her neck.

"Caroline Morton!" she exclaimed. "You shall know when I choose to tell you, and not a minute sooner."

"That was not a no." Caroline responded. "And it is Caroline Wexford now, remember."

"How strange that is to think of." The two older women turned to the younger one, curiosity on their faces. "Well, Mama was once a Wexford and became a Morton, and now you have done it the other way around."

"It is not that odd when you remember half of the aristocracy does the same. It is how the Hapsburg's ended up with that jaw, at least I am not related to Duncan by blood, unlike them."

The Hapsburg jaw? Dear lord, Caroline was definitely spending too much time with the man!

"That is another thing. You husband is only two years younger than your mother."

"He is still only six years older than me!" Caroline protested. "Once again, it does not really make a difference because Mama is really our stepmother."

"Oh, I know. I just find it interesting, is all."

"You sound like Eliza. She brought it up the other night how we are related three times over."

Caroline did not think of how that comment would garner interest for another reason until it was too late. She cringed as she saw the look her mother and sister shared with one another.

"Are you becoming friendly with her?" Anne asked in a faux-innocent voice.

"As we are related three times over, it is only natural that we should meet."

"And she does not mind?"

"Mind what, Mina?"

"Oh, you know, the Harry thing."

"There is no Harry thing."

At that, the younger women let out a laugh. Caroline was grateful when their mother loudly shushed her.

"Are you honestly telling me that your prior infatuation with Harry Wexford has no influence on your relationship with his wife at all?"

Listening to her sister's question, Caroline felt the familiar confusion begin to emerge. Her gaze darted between the two women, who appeared to go through an entire array of emotions upon seeing her face.

What started off as amusement turned to confusion, then disbelief, which in turn became concern.

"Caroline sweetheart," Anne cautiously began, "your feelings for Harry have dissipated, have they not?"

Feeling her lip begin to tremble, she tried to keep her composure, but her Mama moving to wrap her arms around Caroline unleashed it all.

"I do not know!" she burst out as the tears began.

For a good five minutes, she continued to sob as her mother offered gentle words of comfort, rubbing her back. Finally feeling as though she had regained a little of herself, Caroline slowly moved out of her mother's embrace, indicating for her to resume her seat.

With a hiccup, she opened her mouth to begin explaining when her sister practically screamed at her to wait. Sending the girl a bemused look, she watched as Wilhelmina rose from her chair, walked to the open doorway and gently closed the door.

Turning back, she shrugged. "I know Duncan is not in, but we would not want to risk anything."

Caroline sent her sister a grateful smile and briefly grasped her hand as she returned to her seat.

With an exhale, she began.

"I was…....I am completely happy with Duncan. As far as I am concerned, our marriage is near perfect."

"However……" her mother's clearly knew what was coming next.

"However," Caroline continued, "there have been moments with Harry that have only contributed to the feelings I bore for him before. It has left me so very confused."

"What sort of moments?" She was surprised by how stern Anne sounded, and one glance at the woman's face reflected that idea.

"Nothing like that!" she quickly shot out. "I mean that there are looks and words shared that seem to me to hint toward a deeper meaning."

Wilhelmina appeared more disbelieving upon hearing that. "Are you sure that he is hinting towards anything of that sort? I imagine you are just misinterpreting his being friendly. It would hardly be the first time."

Caroline shook her head. "I know that he would not wish to be outright considering the circumstances, but I am certain this is different."

The other women once again shared a meaningful look, and she knew they did not have the same opinion as her own.

"Sweetheart," Anne softly spoke, "I do not wish to tell you that what you feel and see is wrong but, from my understanding, Harry is completely besotted with his wife."

"Even if it were the case that he thinks of you like that," Wilhelmina added, "you are married to his brother. Any sort of affair would be catastrophic."

"You think that I do not know that?" She was incredulous at the thought of their even thinking that she would do such a thing. "I have no intention whatsoever of straying from my husband, and certainly not with his own brother!"

Both women shirked back at Caroline's outburst, forcing her to calm herself.

"There is no one dearer to me in this world than Duncan but that does not mean that I can control how I feel. That is what is confusing me, why I should feel such a way when every other moment of the day, I am blissfully happy."

"Are you?"

Caroline leaned back at her sister's question. She knew with every inch of her being that Duncan was the perfect match for her.

Her mother was right, there was a comfort there that she had never felt before, and, though she felt these confused feelings when in the presence of her husband's brother, Duncan had become her whole world.

He was her friend, her lover, her confidant (on most matters), and most of all, Caroline felt when in his presence an ease and contentment that no one else could provide for her.

She did not wish to jeopardise that, and what's more, there was nothing really tempting her to do so. All there was

was a handful of looks and words which flared up a passion from before.

It was interesting, she thought, that once upon a time she would not have cared for anything if Harry had given her those signs. She would have become his mistress without a moment's hesitation.

But now she did not want to. She just wished that light fluttering of her heart would stop when near him.

Chapter Twenty-Three

Though she was feeling a little stiff, Caroline was determined not to move a muscle. She was far too comfortable lying in her husband's arms.

Thinking to herself, she decided that this was her favourite time of day: After she and Duncan had gone to bed, engaged in the most enjoyable acts and then simply lay there, revelling in post-coital bliss.

She let out a light breath, perfectly content to remain in this position until she fell asleep.

"What was that for?" his deep voice rumbled from above her head.

"What?"

"The sigh."

Caroline smiled to herself, reaching her hand up to pat his cheek.

"I was wondering if I should say 'good sport' for another job well done."

"If you think that I find what we just did a job, you have been paying very little attention."

"How can I possibly pay attention to you whilst you are doing so much to me?"

Caroline rolled onto her front to face him and began absentmindedly toying with the hairs on his chest.

"Perhaps I should start being selfish when I take you to bed from now on." Duncan responded, looking down at her with a smirk.

"Oh yes." she played along. "I imagine it is such pressure to have to maintain a reputation such as yours."

"It is positively exhausting."

"It must be such a relief to have had a reprieve from it all these past weeks. Even if it is only temporary."

His eyes narrowed at her. "What is that supposed to mean?"

"A man in such high demand must keep up appearances." Caroline responded. "Or have you already returned to your scandalous ways?"

At that, Duncan lifted his torso, resting his elbows on the bed for balance as he looked down at her with a serious face.

"Why the devil would you think that I am engaging in love affairs?"

Now it was Caroline's turn to sit up, rising onto her knees.

"Whyever should I not? You are Duncan Wexford after all."

"What does my name have to do with anything?"

Caroline shook her head in a mixture of annoyance and amazement.

"Perhaps not your name, but most certainly your reputation. Everyone expects you to continue with your affairs."

Duncan ran his hands over his face. "I do not give a drat what anyone in this universe expects except for you and I find it rather frustrating to hear that my wife just assumes I shall stray."

Her jaw dropped as the meaning behind his words properly hit her.

"You mean to say, that you have not had any affairs since we wed, and nor do you intend to have them?"

"For god's sake Caroline, we make love three times a day at least, when should I ever find the time or energy to take a lover?"

Utterly gobsmacked, Caroline stared at her husband, searching his face for any hint that he might be playing a joke on her. Finding no such suggestion, she let her truly feelings be known.

"How could you do such a horrid thing to me?" she scolded, causing his eyes to widen in surprise.

"My being a loyal husband is a horrid thing? What sort of thoughts has my cousin been filling your mind with?"

"Do you not realise the implications of all this? And how they shall affect me?"

"Oh please, do tell." He lay back down again at that, crossing his arms and looking particularly pouty.

"For one thing, all of your needs have now been set at my feet." Caroline did not miss his tut at that. "I am quite serious. With no other lovers in sight, the responsibility of pleasing you is entirely on me."

"You do see how ridiculous you sound? I have no reason to wish to stray. We are enjoying one another. Is that not the whole point of it all?"

Caroline grumbled that she conceded that point, as much as she wished not to.

"But I still believe it is pressure to not bore you at all."

"Is life not just trying to keep ourselves from boredom to begin with? OW!"

His pained reaction to her smacking his arm made her feel a little better.

"That is not my only point, though."

"Very well, Lady Duncan, please go on." His casual demeanour and the way he waved his hand for her to continue only served to inflame Caroline further.

"Will you at least try to pretend you are taking this seriously?" she snapped.

"When you put forth valid arguments I will."

Caroline let out a loud huff, making him laugh. Unsurprisingly, it did little to help her mood improve.

"Fine!" she started. "Then what about the societal pressures you shall be putting upon me?"

"I have no clue what you are talking about."

"Women will have a contempt for me for stealing you away. I shall be on the end of a barrage of dirty looks and barbs from all of them. Not to mention that everyone in the ton will be staring at me, anyway, trying to discern what makes me so special to tempt you into fidelity."

Duncan barked out another laugh at that.

"Everyone would already be looking at you because you are the most beautiful woman in London!" That surprised her. "And any women who would stare daggers at you or insult you in any way would not be the sort of woman I should want in my bed anyway."

"Oh." Caroline could not think of any other way to respond.

"Why should any of this surprise you? I thought we agreed how well this marriage suited the both of us?"

"Well, yes." She felt very awkward now. "I had thought that it included my understanding of your affairs, though."

"Clearly, there has been some miscommunication somewhere."

"It is quite obvious where." They shared an awkward smile at that. Duncan's quickly faded, though, and a look of uncertainty crossed his features.

"Now that you know where I stand on this matter, might I ask of your own thoughts?"

Her nose crinkled in confusion.

"My thoughts?"

"Yes," one hand came up to massage his neck, "I mean do you intend on having any affairs of your own? You have mentioned it before."

"I have," Caroline agreed, then added thoughtfully, "I suppose it was all hypothetical, though. I do not really feel the desire nor the need to find someone else."

"Well, darling. Now that is precisely how I feel."

"How fortunate that we have both come to the same conclusion," she joked, "albeit with some confusion along the way."

"Most definitely." Duncan nodded in agreement. His eyes then turned dark. "Now, I think you should come here and kiss me to make up for the worry you just put me through."

"That was hardly anything to cause you much concern." Caroline protested, but still moved to lean over him.

Taking his mouth with hers, she kissed him languidly, simply revelling in the feel of him. Coming up for air, she rested her forehead against his.

"Do you really think me that beautiful?" she shyly asked.

Duncan's hands rose to cup her face and she melted into their hold.

"I do not think I could put into words how I truly think of you."

Swallowing a lump in her throat, Caroline tried to will herself to not melt into a puddle at her husband's declaration.

It was moments like this, when they were alone and tender with one another, that caused all her little confused ones to fade to dust.

Caroline may be foolish at times, but she was not a fool. She really was the luckiest girl on the planet to have this irritant as her husband.

Forcing down her sentimental thoughts, she wickedly grinned and moved to straddle her husband. Judging by the hardness she felt press against her backside in reaction, Duncan had no complaints.

"I think you can find a way other than words to show me."

For a moment, Duncan remained still, his brows lifting in interest at her challenge and Caroline began to worry that she had done the wrong thing.

The squeal she let out once he pounced on her said otherwise.

Three hours later, Duncan was still awake.

Caroline had fallen asleep an hour earlier, gently nestled in his arms. He had known the moment she drifted off by the feel of her body loosening and the way her breathing evened out.

Each night was much the same. He had realised as time went on that he was recognising more and more things about her.

In this case it was when her body drifted into slumber. At other times, it was different.

He knew when she ate that if her lips pressed together tight for a moment, it was because she was savouring the taste.

He knew when they were with her family that her eyes glistened as she listened to her brother.

He knew that earlier, when he laid part of his feelings bare, and admitted how beautiful he thought she was and how he intended to be loyal to her, that she felt perfectly content in their marriage.

Every look, every movement, it all made him fall in love with her more each day.

The only problem was that he also knew, when they were in the company of his own family, that her every thought lingered on his brother. There was a blind adoration in her eyes that he had never felt resting on him.

On every occasion, it had ripped his heart into pieces. He was even debating whether to limit how often they spent time with his family, no matter how much he adored them.

In the end, he realised it was of no use. He would have to settle for his marriage remaining the way it had been. It was not so bad, all that was missing was love on her part, after all.

The one thing that Duncan did not know, was if it would be enough.

Chapter Twenty-Four

"Duncan, I need you to move a little closer to Matthew." He grumbled as he followed his mother's direction.

The entire Wexford family was gathered in his parent's gardens, huddled on the lawn with their backs to the house. He had only been made aware of it the day before, when Caroline had informed him over lunch that his mother was expecting them for a portrait sitting.

"Are you certain that this is best?" he spoke a little clearer, determined to swap the position she had placed him in.

For some ungodly reason, the Duchess had decided it best that the men gather on one side, whilst the woman stood on the other. They were all lined up behind his parents, who sat on chairs trying to keep their squirming grandchildren in their arms.

"What you mother says, goes." his father answered back, making Duncan cross his arms like a petulant child.

"I just think it would appear better to have each couple beside one another, not apart this way."

"Why are you even trying to reason with them?" Matt muttered next to him. "Give me one example of a project Mama has gotten into where she has been convinced to change her mind."

"Finding a wife for our brother." Duncan elbowed his younger brother in the ribs for that.

"Steady on, old man." Harry said. "You just attacked a cripple."

"You are only a cripple when you decide the situation calls for it."

"Might I remind you, Xander, that the only reason I have for being nice to you is because you are married to my sister. You are treading awfully close to knocking down my resolve."

Turning his head to the right, Duncan shared an amused smile with his brother-in-law, who knew just what to say to Harry.

"You are forgetting that your wife is also like a sister to me." He winked at Duncan. "I think she might have something to say if you try anything."

For a moment, Harry looked as though he would offer a retort to that but seemed to think otherwise as his defiant look contorted into one of consideration, and he nodded at the older man.

"Fair enough."

Duncan could not help but bark out a laugh at that.

"This is where I went better than the rest of you." Matt said on his left.

"Dare I ask?"

"Simple," he grinned. "I was the only one of our siblings to have to common sense not to marry into the Ainsworth family."

"I do not think Connie and I have technically married into the Ainsworths." Duncan reasoned.

"But in every other sense you have."

"And quite right, too." Harry shot back. "Life has been a great deal more fun since we brought the Ainsworths into the fold, do you not think?"

"I think that if Caroline hears any of you refer to her as an Ainsworth, you will not be long left for this earth." Duncan snarked, his irritation quickly returning.

"What are you all talking about?" The sound of his wife's voice made all four men turn. She stared at them all with suspicion in her eyes.

"Your husband was just saying how enjoyable he has found it having married into the Ainsworth family."

Duncan cringed upon hearing his younger brother's words. He frantically shook his head at his wife in denial. She did not appear to believe him.

"I am going to suffer for that tonight." he prodded Harry's waist as the men resumed their discussion.

"I hope so." the younger man smirked. "Your marriage thus far has been far too easy."

"Just because the rest of you could not manage to be good husbands......."

His voice drifted off as a commotion broke out in front of him.

"Oh hell." he heard Xander murmur before breaking into a bellow. "UNA GET BACK HERE RIGHT NOW!"

Duncan's three-year-old niece had managed to break free of her grandmother's hold and was already halfway back to the house. Duncan and his brother's all burst into laughter as they watched their sister and brother-in-law, along with several footmen chase after the speedy child.

"Oh dear," his mother said behind him, "if she reaches the house, we shall certainly not finish this portrait today."

Duncan sobered up a little at the thought of spending more than one day just standing around as the artist failed to create his likeness.

"Do you remember last time?" Eliza asked. "She had found such a good hiding spot that she we could not find her for at least three hours."

"We could not find her at all!" Jane said. "She just wandered into the kitchen out of nowhere asking for biscuits."

"That is a girl after my own heart." Harry gleefully proclaimed.

It seemed that the eldest grandchild's escape had set off the rest of the group, as soon enough the gardens were filled with the sound of four screaming infants.

"I believe it is time for this little one's nap." Jane cooed at her son, taking Edmund into her arms.

"I agree." Eliza commented, emptying the Duke's arms of his other grandson before depositing him into Caroline's arms. "You do not mind taking him, do you?"

"It is too late now." Duncan thought his wife may have sounded protesting, but she could not hide how enthralled she was with the toddler.

He watched as she followed Eliza and his mother to the house to settle down the children. She had far more tolerance for infants than he did, it appeared.

"What a shame." he sarcastically exclaimed, clapping his hands together. "We shall have to end this little session for the day."

"Do not even think about it Duncan Wexford!" his mother called out to him. "You boys can still be drawn."

The simultaneous groan of the three brothers filled the air. Chuckling, their father rose from his chair and began to walk away.

"Where do you think you are going? That includes you!" Matt yelled after his father, who did not stop in his steps.

"I am not a boy." he called back.

His three sons stared after him, decidedly unamused.

"Please tell that when you are Duke," Duncan said to his older brother, "you will not be that mean."

"I think if leaving us to sit for a portrait when we are all grown is the worst thing Papa has done, we should be very thankful, indeed."

"You are no fun." Duncan had to agree with his younger brother.

"If you please, My Lords, I shall need to see your faces."

The three men turned back to face the artist, a Mr Baines, who was looking at them nervously. No wonder, Duncan thought, as his mother had a penchant for engaging the services of unestablished craftsmen. The man had probably never met an aristocrat in his life. Today he had been confronted with ten of them!

Resuming their poses, not a single smile graced the lips of the brothers, as each one appeared less amused than the next, despite how Mr Baines tried to encourage them to relax.

"How long do you think this dratted thing shall take?" Matt muttered under his breath.

"Hours I imagine." Duncan winced at Harry's proclamation. "Eliza had one commissioned for us a month ago. My back still hurts."

"That is the most devastating thing you have ever said, little brother." He just wanted to go home with his wife. As usual, Duncan had very little luck.

"Lord Henry, could you place your hand on your brother's shoulder please?" Mr Baines called out. Harry cursed under his breath as he complied.

"What are your plans once the season ends?" Matt asked. The final ball of the season would take place in six days' time, and it could not come fast enough for Duncan. A first for him.

"We shall be going straight to Cumbria." Harry answered. "I believe we shall not join the family until the yuletide."

"Edmund will be beside himself at not being able to follow after Patrick anymore."

"He has only just turned one," Duncan said to his older brother, "he shall forget he has a cousin soon enough."

"It is the time before he forgets I dread." Matt fired back. "You shall see."

"I am delighted to say that I shall not." Duncan smirked.

"Whyever not?"

"I plan on surprising Caroline with a belated wedding trip."

"And there was me thinking you were planning to find yourself a little farmhouse where you could hide her away from the rest of us."

Duncan froze at Harry's suggestion. He thought for a moment that his brother was bringing his greatest fear to life. The fear must have been evident in his face, as Harry's brows furrowed in confusion at him.

"Is it that surprising, brother? You undress her with every look."

He let out a sigh of relief.

"Yes," Matt agreed, "I think we all expect you to lock her up and enact your wildest fantasies for however long you wish."

"I suppose my wife has no say in this?"

Matt snorted. "She looks at you the same way you look at her. I think you may end up running away from her in the end."

Duncan rolled his eyes. "Trust me, that will *never* happen."

Both brothers burst into riotous laughter at that. No matter how Mr Baines tried to rein them in, he simply could not do so."

"Who would have thought it?" Harry asked, wiping a tear from his eyes.

"Thought what?" asked Duncan, irritated.

"You would think that with the number of times we have told our smitten brother that he is so smitten, it would have sunk in by now." Matt smirked to Harry, much to Duncan's chagrin.

"You know, little brother, I think you may have had a point earlier about my being the only one of us with a good marriage." he retorted.

"Nice try, Dunc." Matt said. "You should just embrace your role as the jester of the family. It is not going to change anytime soon."

"Never."

"On that note." Harry started. "MR BAINES, WE ARE GOING BACK TO THE HOUSE."

"Why are you shouting?" Duncan asked, confused.

"He is already terrified of us. He just needed a little push."

Duncan may not have been keen on his younger brother's methods, but he could not complain at being able to get out of the sun at long last.

The three men made their way back into the house to find the rest of the family happily relaxing in the parlour, feasting on cakes.

"Hmmm." came Matt's disapproving reaction which Duncan wholeheartedly agreed with.

"I did not think you would be back so soon." the Duchess remarked.

"Clearly." Harry responded, forcing his wife and Caroline to move as he sat between them. Duncan moved to perch on the edge of the chaise by his wife, keeping one eye on how close his brother remained.

Their mother sent her youngest son a disapproving look. "Now that you are here, I was saying that I plan to make this a tradition."

"Make what a tradition?" Matt asked.

"Having a family portrait painted." *Oh joy!* "Now that your brother is married, I believe it would be lovely to have one made every year to show our growing family."

With that, the other four men in the room turned to stare at Duncan, who flinched at his mother's words.

"This is why none of us like you." Harry glared, ignoring the protests of the women.

Before he could even make an attempt to protest, small conversations broke out in the room, rendering anything he could say unheard.

"If it helps, I still like you." Caroline prodded his leg as she spoke.

"Good." Duncan smiled. "Yours is the only opinion that matters to me."

An uncertain look came across Caroline's face. He indicated his head for her to speak.

"I just had a feeling earlier." She bit her lip for a moment and Duncan wondered what his wife could possibly be so nervous about. "It surprised me how much I enjoyed being with the children."

Duncan felt a minor tinge of panic arise, though he was not sure why. For all he knew, Caroline was with child already.

"You are better than I am, then." he confessed. "I have always found children to be rather tedious." The hurt look that crossed her face caused him to panic, and he quickly sought to rectify it.

"But I shall like our ones." he whispered, overjoyed to see her grateful smile.

He supposed it was true, in any case. Their children would be better.

As long as they hired several nursemaids. They would be the product of him and Caroline, after all.

Chapter Twenty-Five

Despite her protestations the previous day, the fact that Caroline and her husband were in attendance of a dinner hosted by the Dowager Duchess of Bristol was a clear indicator that she was considered a part of the Ainsworth family.

In fact, Anne had advised that Liam's mother had been rather insistent that her daughters join them. Naturally, Duncan had not been able to resist making some teasing remarks during the carriage ride to the Dowager Duchess' Mayfair residence, but soon began to behave once they were in the house.

Truthfully, Caroline thought he might still have some residual feelings of uncertainty left over for the family from their days as rivals. Even if it had all been put behind them.

"I am beginning to suspect a conspiracy is afoot." Harry said from his seat on her right.

The dinner party was larger than the Wexford's owing to the immediate Ainsworth family considered to be the Dowager Duchess, her four children, her stepdaughter, two son-in-law's, one daughter-in-law, two 'granddaughters' and their husbands. If the Earl of Sutton and Mr Robert Calvert had been in attendance as unofficial members of the family, they might have had to move the table to the ballroom or gardens.

Caroline had been placed right in the middle, between Harry and Lord Freddie Ainsworth, who had not spoken a single word to her and whom she found to be a little standoffish.

"I cannot wait to hear." she eagerly responded, grateful to sit next to someone she felt comfortable enough with. "I imagine it shall be as outlandish as ever."

"I may disappoint you there." he feigned sympathy. "Have you noticed, Caroline dear, that at every dinner party we attend, the pair of us at sat beside one another?"

Caroline had noticed that but was reluctant to think too hard on it.

"It had crossed my mind. I simply thought it a small coincidence."

"That is what I thought at first, but then I considered how unlikely it was." he pointed his finger at her to emphasise his point. "Just look at how many different seating combinations there are. I find it very suspicious."

Trying not to laugh at the serious, thoughtful look on the man's face, she suggested the most logical solution.

"Let us discount your family dinner for obvious reasons."

"They are less obvious than you think. Why are we not considering them?"

"We were a smaller party then; it was almost inevitable that we would be sat next to one another."

"I shall give you that."

"How kind." she sarcastically replied. "But regardless, I think the seating arrangements tonight may be a sign of our hostess' kindness."

Harry frowned for a moment as he considered her point, then his eyes widened, and he nodded in agreement.

"And she thought to seat you with someone you were more familiar with." he voiced her conclusion well.

"Mina and I are both unable to be seated by our husbands, therefore yourself and our stepfather were left over." Caroline indicated her head to her sister, who was seated to the left of Liam's seat at the head of the table.

"Now this is why I maintain that you are the smartest person I know."

Caroline felt her cheeks flush at the complement. Once again, Harry was managing to bring her emotions back to that of the smitten girl of her younger years.

"Just do not tell your husband I said that." he whispered. "I should not wish to incur his wrath."

She managed to voice some uncaring response, but all Caroline could think was that it simply continued her own conspiracy about the double meanings behind his words.

"Tell me, Miss Caroline, how do you feel being in the thick of the lion's den?"

"I think the Ainsworth's have a worse bark than bite." she gleefully whispered back. "And may I remind you that I have not been 'Miss Caroline' for almost a month."

"I shall never think of you any other way."

"What are you two whispering about?"

Caroline's head whipped round at her mother's question, distracting her from her brother-in-law's sincere gaze and her own fluttering heart.

"We are scheming, obviously." Harry casually answered from her side. Her mother sent her a look that was both suspicious and disbelieving. Clearly Anne still did not see what Caroline had.

"Oh joys." Liam's sister, Colette, remarked. "We have another pair on our hands. Along with Eliza and Freddie, I doubt we shall ever feel completely at ease now."

"You forgot to name yourself and Liam in that point, dear." the Dowager Duchess told her daughter. Caroline was not surprised to learn that Liam had a mischievous streak in him and said as much.

"People tend to forget because he is the serious Duke now." Freddie finally deigned to speak to Caroline.

"People are the same with Matt." Harry answered, "Everyone considers him to be the dull heir and are surprised to hear of the trouble he got into when we were children. Did he not fill your bedsheets with sand on one occasion, brother?"

"Yes."

Caroline was a little bemused by her husband's blunt response. She sent him an enquiring look, but he chose to ignore it and resumed consuming his meal, ignoring the conversation around him.

On any other occasion, Caroline would be eagerly participating in a debate over how a child would get hold of a large amount of sand in the middle of London, but she was more concerned over her husband's manner to think of it.

For the remaining three courses, Duncan did not say a single word more, heightening her worries and preventing her from actively engaging in her own conversations.

Harry tried several times to draw her back into another conspiring discussion, but she was only able to half-heartedly reply.

Once dinner had finished, Caroline reluctantly followed the rest of the women in retreating to the parlour, sending her husband a final lingering look as she left.

Graciously accepting a glass of port from her hostess, she moved to sit in the armchair beside her sister, anxious for a little form of comfort as she waited for the men to join them.

Hopefully, she would be able to question Duncan without garnering attention.

"How are you finding our new family?" Wilhelmina asked quietly.

"They all seem pleasant."

"But you have been too distracted." her sister observed. Caroline glanced over to find blue eyes boring into her.

"I cannot help it if I have my own concerns."

"No, but you do need to focus your gaze onto something other than another man." Caroline was confused by her sister's scolding.

"What?"

"I do not think anyone else noticed but," Wilhelmina's eyes darted around the room to ensure no one was listening before lowering her voice, "you need to consider that soon other people will see how you are looking at your husband's brother."

"Oh." Caroline answered. "I had entirely forgotten about Harry." She then felt rather defensive, having spent a good deal of dinner worried after her own husband. "I could hardly help talking to him, I was sat next to him, after all."

"It was not that you were talking to him, but how you looked at him. You are truly quite lucky that only Mama and I know of your feelings at this time."

"At least someone does. I do not even have a clue."

"Can I offer you some advice, then?" Wilhelmina did not even bother waiting for her sister to answer. "As simple as this sounds, you need to forget about *him* and focus on your husband."

"Do you think I have not been doing that? I have already told you that it is only when I am in *his* presence that I ever think about him. Otherwise, my mind is entirely focused on Duncan."

Caroline did not get the chance to hear her sister give another rebuttal, as their attention was taken by the Ainsworth sisters, who were trying to drag them into their teasing.

"Come along, girls." Eliza joked. "I am certain you can confirm how my brother is an utter bore for your mother."

"Just remember that the rest of us shall never agree if you try to defend our brother." Colette grinned.

"As the ones who were forced to live with them," Wilhelmina answered, "trust us when we say that they are both as bad as each other."

"Just wait until you have your own children," Anne shot back, "then you will see how dull they find you to be."

"I am certain I can find a way to impress them." Caroline shook her head at her sister's defiant attitude.

"I cannot wait to see you disappointed, Mina dear."

"I am afraid I already have fallen to the curse." Colette said. "I told Oliver to pick up his toys and he sent me the filthiest look in return."

"I am sorry to inform you, darling, but I recall you doing the same at that age." Colette scowled as her mother sympathetically patted her shoulder.

"It has been funny watching Liam have to play the father to two young ladies, though." Marie contributed.

"It is funny having to watch Liam do anything other than be serious." Eliza replied.

"As loathe as I am to say it," Caroline admitted, "he was faced with a rather unique situation."

"Precisely." Anne joined in, eager to come to her husband's defence. "When you consider that he has only needed to worry about it for three months, I think he has come out unscathed."

"For now."

"That was a little sly, Mina." Caroline said with suspicion.

"We may have wed quickly." Her sister's voice was sickeningly sweet. "But just remember, being a father to two unmarried girls for a brief time is far different to being a father to a young child......or a grandfather."

Caroline could not stop the amused smile from emerging at that thought. Judging by the looks of all the other women in the room, they felt very much the same.

"Dear lord, I do not want to know what you all were talking about." Freddie said, leading the men into the parlour.

Ignoring the continued conversation, Caroline eagerly stared at the door, waiting for the handsome figure of her husband to emerge.

Surprisingly, he did not. Instead, his younger brother headed straight for her, ignoring his own confused wife in the process.

"What has gotten up my stupid brother's backside?" he asked her in a low voice.

"Where is he?"

"He wandered off saying something about needing to relieve himself."

Caroline hoped he was speaking truthfully.

"What has happened?" she asked.

"He has been sulking the entire night." Harry was looking more worried than anything. "I tried to ask him if all was well after we finished our cigars, but he just snapped at me and walked off."

"I kept trying to catch his eye during dinner, but he would not look at me once."

"I normally would not be too concerned but I have never seen him behave this way in public before."

"Come along, Harry," she tried to reason, "this hardly counts as public."

"Either way there are people outside of the family present. Duncan does not show himself to his true family half the time."

Caroline nodded in agreement, growing ever more concerned. She almost jumped upon feeling his hand come to rest on the back of her chair, accidentally brushing against her shoulder.

At least she thought it was.

"Promise me you will ask him tonight?" Harry pleaded. "Please try to reason with whatever nonsense he has in his head."

She nodded once more; her eyes locked with Harry's. He was the first one to break the gaze, turning to look across the room. He started in surprise.

Caroline followed his gaze and saw that Duncan had finally joined them. She shirked under his steel gaze, unable to tell what could possibly be going through his mind.

Willing herself to send him a reassuring smile, she watched as he made his way over to them and nudged his brother out of the way.

As Harry began to move to Eliza's side, he shared a concerned and bemused look with Caroline. Her eyes quickly returned to her husband, who remained frowning.

"Is anything amiss?" she asked, hesitantly.

He looked down at her, and his face softened, prompting Caroline to let out a breath she did not realise she was holding.

Duncan's hand came to rest on her shoulder, gently rubbing it with his thumb. She found herself leaning into his touch.

No doubt he would tell her what was wrong when they returned home. Caroline was certain that, whatever it was, it was not serious.

Chapter Twenty-Six

"The game is exceptional in the Autumn months. I imagine you shall find it so yourself."

Caroline had the keenest sense that history was repeating itself. It was the final ball of the season, she was dancing a waltz in the arms of Mr Woodward, who was recounting his last visit to the Wexford's country estate.

"I cannot say that I will be partaking in the hunt, but I imagine I shall find many other features that shall entice me."

The man smiled down at her in approval. She found it interesting how much more at ease she felt dancing with him when the prospect of marriage was out of the question.

"Might I be frank, Lady Duncan?"

"As long as it is not too scandalous." Caroline teased and was surprised by the amused smile on the man's face. Apparently, once a woman was married, men felt more comfortable with her.

"Do you recall the last time we danced?"

"It was the O'Neill ball, was it not?" He nodded in confirmation.

"Once our dance had ended," he started, "you rushed off and the next time I saw you, you were dancing with Lord Duncan."

A small smile fell upon her lips at the memory. He was so irritated at the time.

"I remember." she answered. "Little did I suspect what would happen next."

"None of us did. I watched the pair of you dancing together and thought it was such a waste of a dance."

Caroline laughed. "I would wager everyone did."

"It is funny how things turn out."

The music drew to a close, and the couple broke apart. Politely curtseying, Caroline thanked Mr Woodward for the pleasant dance.

"It was my pleasure, Lady Duncan." He was silent for a moment and appeared to be having a debate in his head. "If it is not too impertinent, I must say that marriage suits you very well."

"I think I agree with you." Caroline nodded.

He then escorted her back to the throng of onlookers surrounding the dancefloor, where they parted ways.

She looked about, trying to spot her husband, whom she was determined to get at least one dance out of. He had spent the entire past week jokingly refusing to even consider the thought of dancing with his wife. Caroline knew he would love to though.

Rising onto her tiptoes, she spotted familiar golden hair near the refreshments, and quickly sidled through the crowd.

"Hallo darling." Eliza greeted her warmly.

"Good evening, did you decide to make up for all the engagements you missed?"

Eliza blinked in confusion, prompting Caroline to nod towards the woman's dress, which was an opulent ruby red.

"Oh!" Eliza exclaimed, nodding. "I have spent the past months being drained out in black over a man I cannot stand. I wanted to wear at least one colourful dress this year."

"If it is any consolation, I thought you looked lovely in black."

The older woman looked intrigued. "And to think that you could not stand me at our first meeting."

"I never said that!" Caroline protested, prompting the older woman to handwave her words.

"Oh please," she laughed, "you did not need to say anything. It was quite clear by the filthy look you gave me."

Caroline was horrified at her prior behaviour towards the woman and fervently apologised.

"Do not fret. Between the animosity between our families and your mother's prior relationship with my brother, I am not surprised at all."

"Well, I am glad that we get along now."

Eliza beamed at that. Her gaze shifted, and Caroline felt a presence come to stand beside her. Looking to her left, she saw that the woman's husband had joined them.

"Miss Caroline!" he joyfully said. "You are looking as lovely as ever."

Her cheeks heated up and Caroline bashfully spoke. "Thank you but I am sure you are exaggerating."

"Nonsense!" he denied. "You are only outshined by my wonderful wife here."

"And he is only saying that out of obligation." Eliza snarkily replied as he kissed her cheek.

"Nonsense!" he said once more. "I am merely terrified of the horrors that should face me once we return home." He winked at Caroline, making her redden even more.

"Now, where is that fool of a brother of mine?" he asked.

"I was wondering that myself."

"I have not had the chance to speak to him since dinner the other day. Has he learnt how to behave again?"

Caroline glanced uncertainly at her sister-in-law; unsure what Harry had told her.

"Have no fear." she reassured. "Harry and I have an unspoken agreement to have no secrets from one another, but anything said in confidence is not to be uttered elsewhere."

Nodding in understanding, Caroline doubted that Harry had told his wife of the feelings she believed he had for her.

"Duncan is being typical Duncan." she explained. "He acted like nothing was wrong when we arrived home and whenever I have tried to bring it up, he……. distracts me."

The couple shared a knowing look and Caroline did not think her face would ever return to its normal colour. She felt it now creeping down her neck.

"Whatever the problem," Harry said, "as long as he stops taking it out on the rest of us, I do not care."

"I am sure that is not true." his wife teased. "You worry more for your brothers than you let on."

"I admit nothing."

Caroline rolled her eyes at his defiance. She took another glance around the room, still with no idea where Duncan had gotten to.

"He will turn up at the end of the night when it is time to go home." Eliza said, looking at her sympathetically.

Caroline did not want to consider what he could be doing in the meantime, forcing herself to remember his promises of fidelity.

"I know." she sighed. "I was just hoping to trap him into a dance."

"You can have the third best Wexford brother instead then."

She tilted her head at Eliza in confusion, wondering if Matt was even present tonight.

"Go along Harry," she continued, ushering her husband along, "I can hold your cane in the meantime."

Caroline and Harry looked at each other uncertainly. She looked back to Eliza, perplexed.

"Is that really wise? Not wishing to offend, but can you dance with a leg missing?"

"Of course, he can," Eliza answered for her husband, "he just cannot do it well. Besides, he is only missing half a leg."

"Yes, but the wooden replacement does not do all the things the last one could." the man in question argued but was shooed away by his wife.

"Go along now." she said as she pushed them towards the dancefloor.

Reluctantly following the older woman's orders, Caroline prayed that no clues as to her true feelings would show on her face.

Curtseying to her brother-in-law, she allowed herself to be taken into his arms as they awkwardly began to waltz. Their eyes met, and the pair promptly burst into laughter.

They were laughing with one another. They were smiling and talking animatedly.

Duncan had only left the ballroom for a moment to relieve himself. The quick trip was prolonged by ten minutes as he was accosted by the wife of a friend and had to gently let the woman down without causing offence.

He thought he did well.

When he had left the ballroom, Caroline had just begun a dance with a Mr Woodson or Woodley or something along those lines.

Upon his return, when he intended to "reluctantly" ask her for a dance, Duncan found she was already engaged in one.

With his brother.

She was gazing at him adoringly.

All Duncan's plans were coming crumbling down. He had made all the arrangements for their belated marriage trip, travelling to Ireland. His hopes were that the time would be spent becoming closer than before.

Then, once they arrived at his parent's estate ready for the yuletide, his wife would be completely unaffected by seeing Harry once more.

If she still appeared just as besotted now, though, after the time they had already spent happily together, Duncan feared that little would serve to lessen her feelings.

"I do not think you could look more miserable if you tried."

For once, Duncan did not squeak at the sudden sound of his sister's voice. He sent Connie a disapproving look, but she simply appeared concerned in return.

"I suggest that we take a turn in the gardens, it is less stifling out there."

"I would prefer not to."

"I am not giving you a choice." Duncan turned to face his sister then.

"You know, you sounded exactly like Mama just then."

"If it gets you to do what you are told, then good."

With that, Connie's hand clasped over his forearm, and she practically dragged him outside.

"Now," she said, slowing them down to a strolling place, "what is your problem?"

"Nothing."

"Duncan Wexford, it is clear on your face that something is troubling you! Now, tell me what it is or I shall be forced to use unspeakable means to force it out of you."

As much as he wanted to remain defiant, Duncan knew that his sister would manage to force it out of him eventually. But he wanted to remain sulking for a little while longer.

"Why should I have to tell you anything?" he petulantly asked. "It is none of your business."

"Believe or not, brother," she halted in her steps and turned to face him, her arms crossed, "I actually care for your happiness, and would gladly help if you would just let me."

He was half tempted to just walk off, refusing any attempts to help him in his life.

"Please Duncan," she said softly, "you helped me once upon a time."

He closed his eyes for a moment, recalling how he did his utmost to help her. But then he had no choice, she was his little sister, after all. It was his job to help.

"Connie," he said, opening his eyes, "this is nothing that I should not have expected."

Her forehead crinkled in confusion, prompting him to go on.

"Caroline and I were never a love match. That she should not return my feelings is not unexpected."

"You have finally realised your feelings then." Connie grinned. "I thought you would never work it out."

"I have known for many weeks now." He admitted,

"Weeks? The rest of us have known for years!" Duncan was incredulous at that.

"Do not be ridiculous!"

"I am not. We all had at least an inkling. You have always been obsessed with her."

"I think obsessed is a little much."

"Whether they were feelings of love or not are inconsequential, you have held these strong feelings for your wife for a good while longer than you realise. Now, why are you so certain she does not feel the same."

Duncan ran his hands through his hair, frustrated.

"Because she is in love with some else!" he protested.

"Who?"

"Harry!"

For a moment, Connie simply stared at him. The disbelief on her face was almost laughable.

"You do know she is not twelve any longer?"

Duncan was not surprised that his sister refused to believe what he was saying.

"I can assure you that if you walk into that ballroom and watch them together, the adoration on her face will be obvious."

"Duncan, you must be mistaken."

"I am not."

"Have you even asked her about this?"

"She would just deny it."

Connie shook her head in disbelief. "You do not know that."

"I think I know my own wife quite well enough, thank you!"

"Fine!" she loudly exclaimed, causing Duncan to look around panicking that their conversation was being heard. "If you will not ask her, then ask him. Harry would assure you otherwise."

"Perhaps I will!" Duncan exclaimed, fed up with it all.

"Good." she nodded, turning on her heel and storming out of the gardens, leaving her brother practically shivering in annoyance and anger.

To his right, Duncan observed a Grecian statue staring down at him, its expression despondent.

"Oh, shut up!"

Chapter Twenty-Seven

Two days. Duncan needed two days to pass without issue and he could whisk his wife away from London and commence his scheme to make Caroline fall in love with him.

What could possibly go wrong?

"Brother!"

He swore under his breath at the sound of his younger brother's voice. Duncan had been under the impression that Harry and his family would have left the morning after the ball for Cumbria. Apparently, he had been mistaken.

"I did not think I would see you here at Whites today." he said as the younger man took the seat beside his, displeasure in his voice. "I had thought you would already be far away from London by now."

"Alas, Liza informed me that our plans had been changed." Harry stole his drink and drained it before he was able to protest. "She is planning on making another matchmaking attempt for her sister."

"Good for her."

Duncan went back to reading his paper, determined to ignore the man beside him. Knowing his brother, this would be a challenge, but Duncan was feeling petty enough to persevere.

"Are your plans still the same?"

Duncan mumbled a confirmation.

"We only have two days left of you then?"

"Mmmhmmm."

"Shall we dine together tomorrow evening?" *No!* "Eliza and I would love to see Caroline and yourself before you depart."

All Duncan could hear was "I would love to see Caroline" and decided that, in record time, he could not bear to spend a minute longer in his brother's presence.

Jumping to his feet, he made his refusals. "My apologies, we have a prior engagement already. If you will excuse me."

With a nod, he turned on his heel and made striding steps to leave the club. He heard Harry calling after him but ignored him.

Walking out of the building, Duncan was relieved to find that his carriage was ready and waiting for him. He would have to pay a little extra to both the coachmen and the club for allowing him to run away from his brother with such ease.

Of course, the fact that the man had half a leg missing helped too!

Diving into the carriage, he hit his fist on the roof and ordered the driver to return home. Feeling constrained, he tore his cravat open.

The second the carriage began to move; an astonishing sight appeared before him.

His brother, a man with half an appendage shot off in the continent and replaced by an awkward wooden replica, had thrust open the door of the moving carriage and bolted inside. Landing on the seat opposite him with surprising grace.

Feeling his jaw drop open, Duncan's head darted frantically between the now closed carriage door and his brother, sat calmly opposite him, casually inspecting his fingernails.

"How did you do that?" he demanded.

"I opened the door and got in."

"I know that!" Oh, the man was irritating! "How did you do that with half a leg missing?"

"You would be surprised what one can do with half a leg missing." Harry straightforwardly replied. "Now, are you going to get that overgrown head out of your backside and tell me what is wrong with you?"

"I do not know what you are talking about." Duncan refused to entertain this conversation.

"You know exactly what I am referring to. You have been a miserable sod for weeks."

"I am perfectly happy."

"You are perfectly frustrating." Harry crossed his arms as he spoke. "There is every indication that you are sickeningly blissful in your marriage, why are you behaving so petulantly whenever I see you then?"

Duncan held one finger up. "First of all, you have no clue what I am like in my marriage." A second digit appeared. "Secondly, I am not behaving in any way other than how I normally do."

"Do you honestly expect me to believe that, brother?"

Duncan wondered if he could get away with throwing his brother out of the carriage without stopping it.

"It is clear as day on every occasion I see you."

He clenched his fist, feeling the sharp sting of his nails against his palm.

"Caroline and I both see it. We are always trying to discern what is amiss with you. She has told me she is just as perplexed."

That did it for Duncan. He saw red and could not hold it in any longer.

"STAY THE HELL AWAY FROM MY WIFE!"

Harry's head darted backwards in surprise and Duncan flinched at the hard sound of his brother's head hit the carriage. Luckily, it appeared to have done him no harm, as it was the one appendage the man could not afford to lose.

For two full minutes, the younger man simply sat there, staring back at him looking completely and utterly gobsmacked.

Unable to take the silence any longer, Duncan finally snapped at him.

"Well, are you going to say anything or not?"

His brother's face contorted into confusion. "I am not entirely certain of what to say."

"You cannot be that clueless."

"I can assure you, I am."

Now it was Duncan's turn to hit his head against the carriage wall. Except this time, it was out of frustration rather than surprise.

Well, maybe a little surprise at how his fool of a brother did not see it.

"Have you not noticed the way Caroline's face lights up when you walk into the room? Or when you smile at her? Or compliment her? Or simply do anything in her presence?"

"Dear god Duncan!" Harry ran his hand through his hair. "Surely you do not think she still harbours that childhood infatuation?"

"I know it."

"You are ridiculous."

"Might I ask how you have come to this utterly ludicrous conclusion?" Duncan grew ever more exasperated at his brother.

"I have just told you!" he found his voice rising above the din from outside the carriage. "It is in every faucet of her behaviour when you are near one another."

"Do you not notice how she lights up when she sees you?" Harry retorted, to his brother's disbelief. "Are you that dim that you do not see how clearly it is how Caroline feels about you?"

If he did not harbour a miniscule of affection for his brother, Duncan would gladly throttle him. Whether for his words of effect on his wife, Duncan did not know.

"For god's sake man, an affection between friends is entirely different from the feelings of love."

"And how would you know?"

"Because I am in love with her!"

Harry simply stared at him in silence. The merest hint of a knowing smile graced his lips. Duncan wanted to punch it off his face.

"I am not going to pretend that confession is surprising."

"Why does everyone have that reaction?"

"Am I the last to hear it from your lips?" Harry asked. "Other than Caroline that is. Or did she spurn you upon hearing it? I doubt that entirely, the girl is too in love with you even if she does not realise it."

"One cannot realise feelings one does not have."

Harry's brows lifted in interest. "Although I thoroughly disagree with that assessment, let us entertain the notion for a moment."

Oh good, little brother is going to act the wise one.

"What are we to do?" he continued. "Am I to forgo any and all association with your wife? We both know that Caroline is too stubborn to allow that."

Duncan had to concede that point. In fact, he thought to himself, if they took any course of action, his wife would soon suspect something was wrong and confront them about it.

"Do you expect me to no longer see you? My own brother?" Harry's voice interrupted his thoughts. "If it meant your happiness, I would do so albeit reluctantly."

"I could never ask that of you."

"Yes, you could." his brother bluntly responded. "When I wed Liza, I knew that I was risking never having an association with any of you again. I've a feeling your love for your wife is the same as mine for my own. You would do so for her, Duncan."

"You cannot compare the two, we would have never given up our familial ties, no matter who you married."

"How was I to know that? The relationship between our two families was so different then, even with Connie's marriage. Just ask it of me, and I will stay away."

"You can stop suggesting it, for I will never ask it." Duncan ordered his brother, his gaze softening to the man.

"Then, what can we do?"

"Nothing."

The carriage jolted to a stop, surprising both men. Duncan lifted the curtain at the window to find that they had arrived at his brother's residence.

"My driver must be good. I never even told him to deliver you home."

"We need to find a solution." Harry ignored the change in conversation. "I refuse to lie down in defeat and accept my brother living in misery."

"Come now, it is not so bad." he protested. "Only when you are around."

Harry did not react to his half-hearted attempt at a joke. He merely grasped hold of his cane and made his way out of the carriage.

Once he had descended onto the ground, he turned back to face his brother.

"I shall think on it tonight and have a solution by the morning. You will hear from me then."

Without saying another word or waiting for a response, he turned and strode into his house, leaving Duncan staring in confusion for a good five minutes after the carriage door had been shut once more and they had begun moving again.

Harry was a determined fellow and creative, he admitted to himself, if any of his relatives could come up with a solution, it was him.

But still, Duncan did not believe it could be resolved. One cannot simply alter another person's feelings, no matter how they tried. It was something that could not be helped.

Otherwise, he would refuse to allow himself to love Caroline so!

Or would he?

Whatever the case may be, things would not change. All Duncan could do was hope that his plans to romance his wife during their marriage trip would succeed.

And even then, he would not know if they had until the family had all gathered in Gloucestershire for the yuletide season.

Resigning himself to his fate, Duncan returned home and greeted Caroline as he normally would. They discussed their preparations to leave London, she tried to pry his plans for their marriage trip out of him, they dined, they made love, they slept.

Then, he was awoken the next morning by a harsh shaking on his shoulder and a hand clasped over his mouth at his protest.

Apparently, his valet had decided he was no longer in need of employment. He put a finger to his mouth and gestured for his master to follow him silently out of the room.

He begrudgingly followed the man into his dressing room, briefly looking back to find his wife sleeping quite soundly. He was never more envious of the woman.

Duncan prepared to begin chastising but was stopped once a note was thrust into his hand.

Feeling an acute sense of foreboding, he opened it and read the brief message.

I HAVE IT!

-H

With a resigned sigh, Duncan lifted his head to speak to the man in front of him.

"I need to dress." he spoke. "It seems I must visit my brother."

Chapter Twenty-Eight

Looking back on her first season, Caroline felt utterly exhausted and wondered if the majority of debutantes had the same feeling or if she was merely an exception.

After all, her season had been rather more eventful than typical ones, she imagined. Her mother wed, causing the family to rise in society, her sister wed, then Caroline had scandalised herself, prompting her own marriage.

And the events were nothing compared to the emotional turmoil and confusion she had undergone!

Needless to say, she was relieved that she and Duncan would be leaving London behind in just one day, leaving her husband's younger brother behind as well.

Caroline fully intended to spend the next few months indulging in all the benefits that came with marriage to Lord Duncan Wexford. She could not wait!

In pure Duncan fashion, however, her husband had decided to leave the house before she had even awoken. No doubt he was making last minute arrangements for their departure, but she still missed him.

He had not returned by the time Caroline had needed to leave to visit her sister, who would be leaving the day after she was.

Looking forward to collapsing into an armchair and not having any more engagements or obligations in the immediate future, Caroline sluggishly wandered into her drawing room and started in surprise.

"Harry!" she exclaimed at the sight of her husband's brother.

The man rose to his feet looking a little less confident than she was used to seeing him.

"I apologize." she offered after regaining her wits. "I was not expecting any visitors today. Is Duncan here?"

"Uh no. I sort of made sure he would not be at home when I arrived."

That intrigued Caroline further. Her eyes flickered to hoe his hands nervously twisted the head of his cane. Motioning for him to sit down again, Caroline took the seat opposite his.

"Should I call for some tea?"

"No!" he hurried out the moment the question left her lips. Briefly closing his eyes, he took a breath a spoke more steadily. "I would rather we not be interrupted."

"Harry, whatever is wrong? You are most unlike yourself."

"In all honesty, I find myself in a position I would never have anticipated before."

Caroline's bewilderment increased. She motioned for him to go on, content to wait patiently for him to be able to voice his worries.

"Well," he rubbed the back of his neck, "would it be scandalous to ask that you close the door?"

She could feel a knot forming in the pit of her belly at that. Hesitantly nodding, she rose to her feet and walked over to close the door. Turning back around, Caroline let out a little squeak upon finding that he had crept up behind her and they were standing inappropriately close.

Swallowing, she saw the serious look on his face and knew what he was about to say.

"I had thought you had forgotten about me." *She had been correct after all!* "Even now, I am torn. I see you and my brother together and think that I am no longer in your favour but then we.........we share these looks."

"Harry......"

"I know that you feel the same."

There it was. Without even saying the words, Harry had confessed that he loved her too. This was the moment she had waited for. Nine years spent hopelessly alone in the belief that he felt the same had finally been justified.

Why did Caroline suddenly feel so sick?

"My love," she could scarcely believe he was using the endearment for her, "I have tried to hide how I feel, knowing that nothing could happen."

Feeling herself begin to sway, she was grateful for Harry's hands coming up to steady her. Though, once she regained her footing, she was endlessly aware of the pulsing hot feel of him pressed against her.

"I can hide it no longer. To be apart from you is a torment."

Her breath began to quicken. What was she to do?

"Whatever you choose, I shall follow you. Whether it be to run away together or never see one another again, I will do as you say, Caroline darling."

Caroline had no clue what to say, though. This was everything she had ever hoped for. The consummation of her love was in front of her, ripe for the taking.

Why did this not feel right, then?

"I do not know quite what to say." she finally managed to get out.

A thoughtful look came across his face, and Caroline's eyes widened as he leaned forward.

"Perhaps we should put our love to the test."

"Harry, what are yo............"

Her words were cut off by his mouth covering hers. Instinctively, her hands rose to press against his chest.

For a brief moment, Caroline gave in to the kiss. Every remnant of the young, smitten girl she once was took over momentarily, indulging in the gentleness of his lips.

A thought then struck her that made her freeze in her movements.

His chest was too firm.

Duncan's was softer. He was not muscled like his brother. Both men enveloped her, but her husband's body was warm and inviting.

From the feel of him, Caroline's thoughts moved onto the kiss itself. Harry was gentle, almost hesitant in his movements. Duncan, on the other hand, would take hold of her as if he would never hold her again.

It finally hit her. Like a sudden bolt of lightning, she saw what she truly desired.

It was not this!

Pushing herself out of his arms, Caroline moved as far away from him as the room allowed.

"I do not want this!" she hurriedly protested.

"Why?"

"Because I am in love with Duncan!"

Her eyes widened in surprise as her hands covered her mouth in shock. Until she had put her feelings into words, she had not realised how great her feelings for her husband were.

"Does that satisfy you now?"

Perplexed by her brother-in-law's response, she looked back at him to find that he was not looking in her direction at all. Following his gaze, her confusion increased as it led her eyes to rest on the window.

About to query him, she was stopped by the movement of the curtains. The blue fabric was suddenly thrust aside by her husband, who had apparently been hidden behind it.

"AHA!" he yelled, rushing to her side, and pulling her to him.

"Have you been behind the curtain this entire time?" Caroline asked, gobsmacked.

"I trust now you will cease being miserable in our company?"

"Yes, yes, now get out of my house."

Caroline tore her gaze back to Harry, who retrieved his cane and left the room, calling behind him that he would see them in two months.

"Duncan, what on earth........."

Her question was cut off by his lips on hers, hard and demanding. As tempted as she was to give in to his ministrations, Caroline needed answers.

Pushing him away, she moved to keep a chair between them.

"Duncan Wexford, you are to tell me what is happening this moment!" she barked at him.

"I thought you were in love with Harry. He believed you loved me. We put it to the test. Now, come here and kiss me."

"Do not dare take one step near me!" she ordered, shocked at the brothers' scheming. Duncan obeyed, to her relief. "Why would you doubt me for one moment?"

He looked at her in teasing disbelief, and Caroline had to concede that it was rather obvious why.

"Fine, but that has no bearing on why you should test me so." Another horrified thought crossed her mind then. "And why did you deem it necessary to bring Harry into this? I shall never be able to look him or Eliza in the eye again."

"If it is any help, it was Eliza's idea in the first place."

"Really?"

"Yes, she thought you needed a push to realise what everyone else could see. The both of us, actually."

Without her noticing it, Duncan had crept around the chair and pulled her to him once more.

"I must say I am delighted to be proven wrong." his voice had lowered to a growl, and a shiver of anticipation crept up her spine.

Nonetheless, she did not wish to give in so easy. They had tricked her, after all. Even if it was a much-needed trick.

"I think I have behaved too rashly." she spoke. "I will go after Harry now."

His arms tightened around her, his smile knowing.

"You do not wish to see my brother."

"I do."

"You love me."

She could not resist breaking into a wide smile to mirror his own.

"And you love me." she returned the sentiment.

"With every inch of my being." he admitted. "I plan to spend every minute of the rest of my life proving it to you."

"Then I shall have to do the same. I should not wish to be less enthusiastic than you."

"I expect nothing less."

Looking into her husband's eyes, everything seemed to make sense to Caroline. All the confusion, all the unknown thoughts and feelings of the past months finally made sense and she wished to waste no more time on uncertainty.

"Now you can kiss me."

Epilogue

December 29th, 1813

"The horse took off like a shot before he had even put a foot into the stirrups. Now, one would think he would have let go at this point but, unlike most people, my brother has no sense whatsoever. He just kept hold of the saddle and somehow managed to flop over the thing, with his behind stuck in the air for everyone in the courtyard to see."

Caroline smiled sympathetically at her husband, who seemed to be taking his brother's teasing in good spirits.

They had returned to London the day before and accepted her mother's invitation to dine with the entire Ainsworth family.

Harry had taken the opportunity to delightfully regale a mishap Duncan had gotten himself into upon their return to Gloucestershire from their marriage trip, which had been spent travelling along half of the English coastline.

Luckily, Duncan had emerged unscathed (he had managed to hurl himself onto his mother's petunias), but his ego was bruised. Especially as the event was witnessed by his brothers.

"I am sure that I can dig up a story of two about you, little brother."

"We all have stories about Harry." Freddie added. "Though when you consider that he has only been in the family for less than three years, that fact is concerning."

"Imagine how many I must have after three and twenty years." Duncan said with a wink.

"Oh god!" the man in question bemoaned, turning to Caroline. "Did you have to marry him?"

She debated for a moment whether to continue teasing her husband. It had appeared that the past months had resolved any misconceptions of her feelings being made, but every so often Caroline had thought she had witnessed a look of uncertain jealousy on her husband's face.

The question was whether to join in with the very men who brought out those feelings.

"Do we all not have horrific stories of our brothers?" Marie pondered, relieving Caroline of risking making the wrong move. "I can safely say that in this family Liam and Freddie are just as terrible."

"Should I take offence at that?" Liam wondered aloud.

"Yes, you should." his brother nodded. "I have just as many stories about the girls."

"Yes, but you would not dare tell them." Eliza responded.

"Why not?"

"Because for every story you tell about us, we have two regarding yourself."

For a moment the youngest Ainsworth siblings had their gazes locked, each one clearly not wishing to give in first.

In the end, it was the brother who relented, raising his glass to his sister with a "fair enough."

The dinner soon descended into rapid tales of sibling antics. Some, mainly Harry and Freddie, were more enthusiastic than others. The quietest had to be Sir Ernest, which did not surprise Caroline, as he knew those present the least. But nonetheless, he gave a good barb or two as he spoke.

"You know, Philpott," Harry's voice broke through the chatter, "I was wondering when I was going to have the chance to meet your mysterious sister."

"You and me both." Colette chimed in, to Caroline's confusion.

"Surely you must be acquainted somewhat with your own husband's sister?" she asked. The blonde shook her head in response.

"She had already vanished by the time I had met Larry."

"I still cannot understand it." Eliza said. "The sister of a baron deciding to go and be a lady's companion. Why would anyone want that?"

"Josephine has always been out of the ordinary." Colette's husband came to his sister's defence. "She simply wanted something different than to just marry and have children."

"One does not have to go into service to escape marriage." Eliza countered. "Just look at Marie. We would never force her off anywhere. She will always be provided for."

"Perhaps that is it." Freddie enthused. "Old Larry here is a cruel brother who will not take care of her."

"Or perhaps he wishes to support her in all she wishes?" Duncan retorted with a firmness that intrigued his wife.

The conversation quickly moved on, but Caroline did not miss the meaningful look her husband exchanged with the Baron. There appeared to be some sort of understanding there.

Nor did she miss the look the Baron then directed at his own wife, who was unaware of his gaze. He appeared rather thoughtful, Caroline imagined, and she could not help but wonder what was running through the man's mind.

Tonight, she decided, she would see if she could pry anything out of her husband regarding The Hon Josephine Philpott.

Eliza was right. Choosing to be a lady's companion was strange. With any luck, Caroline would uncover the mystery by morning.

If not, she would enjoy herself with her husband very much indeed.

COMING SOON

Risking Her Ruin

Lady Colette Philpott had never considered herself anything out of the ordinary. She had done her duty: marrying and having children, including an heir for her husband's title. Unlike the marriages of her brother and sister, there was no great love between herself and her husband, but there was a great affection. Overall, she was happy with her perfectly ordinary life. At least, she was until her husband's sister came to visit….

Josephine Philpott was lost. She had known when she had left the safety of her family to be a lady's companion, it would not last forever. It had caused chaos and confusion and she did not know how she would have managed it without the help of her little brother, the only person who knew her secret. To the rest of the world, she had lost an employer when, in reality, she had lost her love. Now it was time to return home in the knowledge that she would not have the chance at such love again. One can only imagine, therefore, how disconcerting it was to meet her brother's beautiful wife….

ABOUT THE AUTHOR

Wed to the Wrong Wexford is the fifth instalment in the Wexford and Ainsworth saga by Laura Osborne. She lives in South Wales with her two precocious kittens.